JN028030

明治を綴る麗しの歌

英語で伝えたい
昭憲皇太后百首

Meiji as Composed in Elegant Verse
100 Poems by Empress Shoken

Harold Wright
Editorial oversight Meiji Jingu Shrine

ハロルド・ライト

明治神宮　監修

中央公論新社

昭憲皇太后御尊影
エドアルド・キヨッソーネ（明治21年）

Official Portrait of Empress Shoken
Edoardo Chiossone 1888

刊行に寄せて

明治神宮宮司　九條道成

『敷島の道に架ける橋──英語で伝えたい明治天皇百首』が上梓されたのは令和四年（二〇二二年）夏、明治天皇崩御百十年目のことでした。そしてこの度、昭憲皇太后百十年祭を迎える令和六年（二〇二四年）四月にあわせて『明治を綴る麗しの歌──英語で伝えたい昭憲皇太后百首』が世に出されることになりました。

明治天皇とそのお后であられた昭憲皇太后を両御祭神とする明治神宮にとりましては、この上ない喜びであります。約三万首残されている昭憲皇太后御歌から選ばれた百首を、流麗なる日本語と英訳とを照らし合わせながら、あるいは英語圏の方々には、五七五七七の韻律に基づく英訳をとおして、その御心と日本文化の粋に触れていただければ幸甚です。

1

アメリカ出身のハロルド・ライト氏が、明治天皇御製、昭憲皇太后御歌を英訳することになった経緯につきましては、既刊の〝明治天皇百首〟に触れられておりますが、明治天皇崩御七十年にあたる昭和五十七年（一九八二年）頃に当時の明治神宮宮司から託されたものをライト氏が大変な労苦をもって三十年以上かけて英訳したものであります。三十一文字という制限の中で日本独特の感性が表される和歌の英訳は、想像し得ないほどの困難が伴うと伺います。本書の刊行にあたっては、改めて明治神宮国際神道文化研究所の佐藤正宏所長が中心となって吟味をし、ひとつひとつの歌から拝することのできる御心を共有し、それにふさわしい英語の表現をジョナサ・ライト夫人とともに練り上げていく、という作業を繰り返された由。御歳九十二歳にしてなお漲（みなぎ）るライト氏の飽くなき探究心と日本文化に対する情熱の賜物であると、改めて敬服申し上げる次第です。

明治天皇あるいはその御治世である明治時代は、多くの皆様方にとって、江戸幕府の終焉から短期間で近代化を成し遂げた輝かしさとともに思い出されることでしょう。一方、その目覚ましい国家形成の中で昭憲皇太后が果たされた御事績には、あまり触れられる機会がないかもしれません。千年に亘る古都京都で守られてきた皇室の伝統を尊重されつつ、明治天

2

皇を内から温かくお支えになられながら革新へと大きく一歩を踏み出された皇后。例えば、宮中に洋装を採り入れられたことひとつとっても、大きなご覚悟を伴われたものと拝察せざるを得ません。開国によってもたらされた西洋文化・文物への女性ならではの眼差しが、いくつもの御歌に表現されています。また、国内産業の振興や女子教育への思い、世界の人々との交流や平和を祈られる御心など、今なお、私たちに優しく語りかけてくださっているかのようです。

さらに心打たれるのは、明治天皇をお慕いになる気持ちに満ちた御歌です。花を手折って届けようとされるお気持ちや、日本各地を行幸される天皇の旅路をご案じになるもの。明治天皇とともに激動の時代を歩まれた御心の内から溢れるように詠まれた御歌をとおして、はしなくも私たちの心の中にもある慈しみや、何気ない自然を愛でて感謝する気持ち、そして受け継がれてきた大和心に思いを馳せていただけることを願ってやみません。

最後になりましたが、長きに亘って英訳に努めてこられたハロルド・ライト氏、そしてジョナサ・ライト夫人に改めて満腔（まんこう）の感謝を表します。また、歌人の永田紅様に玉稿を賜りましたことに衷心より御礼申し上げます。

目次

刊行に寄せて　　　　　　　　　　　　　　　　　　　　　　1
　　　　明治神宮宮司　九條道成

まごころの和歌――昭憲皇太后の御歌　　　　　　　　　　9
　　　　詩歌翻訳者　ハロルド・ライト

〈解説〉皇后の心を写す三万首　　　　　　　　　　　　　29
　　　　歌人・細胞生物学研究者　永田　紅

昭憲皇太后百首　　――日英併記――　　　　　　　　　　49

カバー　御小袿
（部分、明治神宮ミュージアム蔵）　撮影 大河内 禎

装　幀　中央公論新社デザイン室

明治を綴る麗しの歌――英語で伝えたい昭憲皇太后百首

まごころの和歌——昭憲皇太后の御歌

ハロルド・ライト

ハロルド・ライト

1931年、アメリカ合衆国オハイオ州デイトン生
まれ。コロンビア大学でドナルド・キーン氏に
師事し、日本語と日本文学を修学。翻訳実績は
幅広く、古代万葉集の和歌から谷川俊太郎の現
代詩にまでわたる。アンティオーク・カレッジ
の日本語学、日本文学・文化学科名誉教授。

明治天皇のお后として

昭憲皇太后は左大臣一条忠香の三女として一八五〇年にご生誕になりました。幼名は勝子、のちに明治天皇とのご婚約に伴い美子と改名されました。このお名前はご本人の淑やかな美しさと小柄なかわいらしさを表したものでした。一八六九年のご成婚のときには明治天皇も皇后もすでに長年に亘り和歌を詠まれていました。和歌は短歌とも呼ばれ、古くから日本の歌人により親しまれてきた三十一音節の形式からなる韻文です。天皇も皇后も共に五歳のときから和歌を詠まれてきました。長年に亘り、お二方は詠まれてきた和歌をお互いに、あるいは皇居の外にご披露になってきました。お若いころの皇后の御歌の一例です。

みがかずば玉も鏡も何かせむまなびの道もかくこそありけれ

If I left unpolished
neither jewels nor mirrors
are worth anything;
this is also very true
of the path of learning.

観菊会

日本研究者として著名なドナルド・キーンの言葉を引用すれば「明治天皇と美子皇后（中略）は子宝に恵まれることはなかったが、（中略）美子は、それ以前のいかなる皇后よりも遥かに傑出した皇后として広く国民に慕われる存在となる」（『明治天皇』角地幸男訳、新潮社、二〇〇一年）。

明治天皇の子供はのちの大正天皇を含め、当時の宮廷の習わしにより他の華族の子女から誕生しています。明治天皇と美子皇后は宮廷の公の場でも私的な生活においても常に睦まじい関係を保たれていました。そのご様子は詠まれた和歌によって知ることができます。

秋ごとにつらなる人の数そひてうたげにぎはふ菊のはなぞの

Viewing Chrysanthemums

Every autumn now,
our invited guests of state
have grown in number;
we have a bustling banquet
in the chrysanthemum garden.

ような皇后の御歌の一例です。

お二方は和気あいあいとした極く内輪の事柄までもたびたび和歌に詠まれています。その

　　花

君がためをらむとすればくろかみの上にみだれてちるさくらかな

Cherry Blossoms

Breaking off a branch
of the blooming cherry
for His Majesty,
petals of flowers are scattered
over our long black locks.

明治天皇と同様に美子皇后の世界観は好奇心に富み、広い心と国際親善を旨としたもので した。また皇后は洋装について革新的なお考えをお持ちでした。「一八八七年の始まりを告 げる新年の儀式は、伝統に則って行われた。ただし、一つだけ例外があった。皇后が初めて 洋装大礼服を着け、宮中の拝賀を受けた。以後、この種の儀式における皇后の洋装は慣例と なった」(前掲『明治天皇』)。

皇后が初めて洋装で公衆の前に現れたのは一八八六年七月三十日、華族女学校(現在の学 習院女子中等科・高等科)に行啓し卒業式に出席された時でした。その後も、外国の要人や 賓客を御引見の際は着物より洋装の方がふさわしいとのお考えをずっとお持ちになっていま

した。

また、皇后は石筆や電報など西洋の利器に魅了されました。

石筆

書く文字のつたなきあともとどまらぬ石の筆こそうれしかりけれ

Slate Pencils

Even if we wrote
something in an unskilled hand
it could be erased;
oh, these "stone writing brushes"
bring us joy of easiness.

テレグラフ

あがたもりをさむる道も一すぢに告げまつるべき糸口やこれ

Telegraph

How do heads of regions
now report to the central office,
the ways they govern?
The clue is in just one thing:
a single thread of wire.

明治天皇御製と共通する三つのタイプ

昭憲皇太后の御歌は明治天皇の御製と同様、次のように分類できます。先ず第一の分類は皇族としての和歌です。皇后としてまた国母としてのお立場から国全体へのお気遣いを詠われたもので、次の三首がその例です。

歳暮

しろしめす大御国内にことなくてくるる年こそそのどけかりけれ

End of the Year

The whole country
under His Majesty's reign
has remained at peace;
and, indeed, the end of this year
is truly calm and tranquil.

五月二十二日みそののながれかれがれになりたるをいかでといぶかりしに苗代
にひきたるなりとのたまはせければ

いかばかりうれしかるらむゆるされてみかはの水を小田にひく日は

Water on the 22nd of May

How happy they must be
the day when farmers are allowed

to draw in water
from the stream in the palace grounds
to flood their own fields of rice.

菫
（すみれ）

里の子がつみしすみれのひとつかねみしらぬわれにおくるうれしさ

Violet

A village child,
without knowing us at all,
granted us a gift
of a bouquet of violets,
bringing us much joy.

二番目の共通の分類は神道に関するものです。この種の和歌は神道の長としての天皇、ま

た神代の時代から連綿と続く皇統の末裔である天皇のお后としての自覚にもとづくものです。

社頭祈世

神風の伊勢の内外のみやばしらゆるぎなき世をなほいのるかな

Prayers at the Ise Shrine for the Reign

At Sacred Ise
we pray at both the Inner
and the Outer Shrines
that, like their pillars,
our reign shall never waver.

三番目の共通の分類は一私人としての和歌といえるかと思いますが、歌人としてお二方の心の底から湧き出る感情の表現として詠われたものです。この種の和歌において皇后がしばしばお詠みになっているのは、御幼少のころに過ごされたお二方の故郷である古都京都のこ

とや自然への愛、特に植物、花、鳥、水について、また知識欲について、そして特に和歌を詠むことへの情熱と喜びについてです。

　　　　冬江

風をいたみ鴨はたちにし水錆江に上毛ばかりぞちり浮かびたる

みさびえ
うはげ

　　　　Winter Bay

As strong winds blew
all the ducks just flew away
from murky waters,
leaving nothing there at all
but scattered floating feathers.

世界平和と国際親善もまたお二方が願われ、共に歌題として採り上げられました。その中の一つに次の皇后の御歌があります。

四海兄弟（けいてい）

もとはみなおなじねざしの人ぐさもことばの花やちぢにさくらむ

Universal Brotherhood

In the beginning
people, like all of our plants,
sprang from one root,
followed by flowers of language
blooming forth by the thousands.

皇后独自の二つのタイプ

明治天皇と皇后が共に採り上げられたこれらの歌題に加えて、皇后はさらに二種類の和歌を詠われていると私は思います。その一つは皇后が天皇に対する個人的なお気持ちを詠われた御歌です。天皇への敬愛とともに数々のご偉業に対する誇らしいお気持ち。これらの多く

の御歌は天皇の御身の上を案じたもので、特に天皇が全国を行幸され、重要な会議、儀式、あるいは国民の幸せを願われた旅先でのことを心配されたものです。

当時は電報や鉄道による手紙の郵送以外にお互いに連絡し合う手段はありませんでした。天皇が行幸されている地方の険しい街道、厳しい気象状況、ご不自由はないか等、皇后はいつもご心配なさっていました。

向が岡にみゆきましましける夜雨いみじうふりいでければ

みくるまを待つまひさしき夕やみにむねとどろかす雨のおとかな

His Majesty's Travel in the Rain

Waiting so long
for His Majesty's carriage
here at nightfall,
this heart of ours is throbbing
to the sounds of the rain.

菊

あれましし日にささげむとおもふかなうゑし垣根の菊のはつ花

Chrysanthemum

We wish to offer
as a Royal birthday gift
the very first bloom
of the hedgerow chrysanthemum
we ourself had planted.

さらに皇后は米国人ベンジャミン・フランクリンが著したいわゆる道徳読本に啓発されて一連の御歌を詠まれています。周知のことですが、皇后は侍講であった元田永孚（ながざね）からフランクリンが下記の美徳を大切にしていたことをお聞きになりました。即ち、節制、清潔、勤労、沈黙、確志、誠実、温和、謙遜、順序、節倹、寧静、公義です。

一九九四年、明仁天皇（当時）は米国へ公式訪問されました。米国大統領はビル・クリントンでした。ホワイトハウスでの歓迎式典で陛下は前述の逸話を披露されています。

次に紹介するのは、美徳「謙遜」についての昭憲皇太后の御歌です。

謙遜

高山のかげをうつしてゆく水の低（ひき）きにつくを心ともがな

Humility

The lofty mountains
are carried in reflection
by flowing waters;
this seeking of humble levels
should be the aim of human hearts.

皇后の御姿につき、華族女学校の英語教師であったアリス・メーベル・ベーコンによる記

24

述が残っています。皇后が彼女の教室を訪れられた時のことです。

私は何度となく皇后のご様子を窺った。そこで目にしたのは小柄で細身の女性で、身に着けられている重厚なはと色の絹のドレスに白い羽が付いたはと色のパリ風ボンネットがやや重苦しそうに感じられた。お顔は寂しげで、その寂しさにじっと耐えているように見受けられた。聞くところによると、皇后は大変理知的なお方で、気丈夫で素晴らしいお人柄であるとのことである。

(A Japanese Interior, Bacon, Alice Mabel, British Historical Print Editions, British Library, 1893)

皇后は長年に亘り西洋の多くの要人やその妻たちをご引見になっています。一八八一年にはハワイのカラカウワ王にお会いになりました。また同年に英国の後の国王エドワード七世の子息たちにもお会いになっています。皇后は米国のグラント元大統領の夫人、ジュリア・デント・グラントを賓客としてお迎えになっています。グラント大統領が退任後の一八七九年に夫妻で行った世界一周の旅の最後に日本に立ち寄った時のことです。グラント夫人は自

叙伝『ジュリア・デント・グラント回顧録』の中で次のように述べています。

両陛下はお立ちになっていました。天皇は御正服を召され、皇后は白い絹のスカートにルビー色のベルベットの宮廷服を召されていました。皇后の御髪はきれいに編まれており、宝石をちりばめた宝冠というよりむしろ孔雀の羽根先に似た羽根飾りをお付けになっていました。皇后はお若くて美しく繊細なお顔立ちでした。皇后は通訳を通して、短く歓迎のお言葉を述べられ、私はそれにお応えしました。

別の機会に皇后はグラント夫人に、長旅の疲れをいたわる慰めの言葉をかけられました。これに対しグラント夫人は次のように応えました。「これまで多くの国を歴訪したが、日本のように親切なもてなしを受けたことはなかった」（前掲『明治天皇』）と。

おわりに

この昭憲皇太后のすばらしい御歌を英訳するという作業は一九六四年の東京オリンピックに際し、明治神宮の髙澤信一郎宮司（当時）から依頼されたのが発端でしたが、思えば大変

26

すばらしく光栄な機会に恵まれたことと痛感しています。

時が経つにつれ、多くの人への感謝の気持ちがますます募ってくるのを覚えます。という

のも彼らはこの美しい御歌の意味を教えてくれたのみならず、その詩的な情緒をいかに英語

で伝えるかということを示唆してくれたからです。

先に私が手掛けた明治天皇の御製を英訳した著書『敷島の道に架ける橋──英語で伝えた

い明治天皇百首』（中央公論新社、二〇二二年八月）では、私がいかにして明治天皇の御製を翻

訳することになったか、また英訳するにあたって、どのような手順を踏んだかなどにつき詳

しく述べましたのでご参照ください。ここで同じことを述べることは差し控えたいと思いま

す。

　先ずもって、明治神宮国際神道文化研究所の佐藤正宏所長とそのチームが東京に於いて、

忍耐強く私とのメールのやり取りに応じてくれたことに感謝します。そしてここオハイオで

は、詩人でもある妻ジョナサ・ハンマー・ライトに感謝したいと思います。彼女はこの本に

関し、用語やアイディアにつき一つ一つ辛抱強く相談に乗ってくれました。私自身九十二歳

となった今日、彼女の未だ若い活力と女性としての洞察力は異文化交流のこの作業遂行に必

要不可欠な助力であったと感じています。

また、誰と言わず、どこでと言わず、私とともに日本とその豊かな和歌の文化について、熱心に対話してくださったすべての方々に対してもここにお礼を申し上げます。それが私の先生であれ生徒であれ、私が愛する人々であれ、本の筆者であれ、あるいは山道で出会った見知らぬ人、または長旅の列車で乗り合わせた乗客だったかもしれません。そんな皆さまはこの本の出版を実現させたあらゆる点において私を支援してくださり、ご協力くださいました。

皆さまは私が日本の和歌を翻訳するというすばらしい人生を歩むことに手を貸してくださったのです。人呼んで「英語」というこの厄介な言葉への翻訳に。

どうもありがとうございました。

〈解説〉

皇后の心を写す三万首

歌人・細胞生物学研究者

永田　紅

昭憲皇太后という響きからまず思い浮かぶのは、大礼服に身をつつみ、星型ダイヤモンドをいただくティアラを着けた肖像写真であろう。明治二十二年（一八八九年）六月に撮影されたこの写真が伝えるように、昭憲皇太后ははじめて洋装をした皇后であった。急速に西洋化を推し進め、近代化をはかった時代にあって、明治天皇の皇后として世の中の劇的な変化に向き合いながら、女子教育や社会福祉に大きな功績を残したことで知られる。そのような

生涯のなかで、約三万首の和歌を詠んでいる。

生家の一条家は由緒ある五摂家のひとつであり、京都御所と道ひとつ隔てただけの場所にあった。京都市内に住んでいる私にとって、御所のある京都御苑は子どものころから身近な場所である。四季折々、いつ訪れてものんびりと心地よい。世界を見回しても、居心地のよい都市にはかならずよい川とよい公園がセットになって備わっているように思うのだが、京都にも鴨川と京都御苑のある幸せをいつも感じるものである。

御苑の北西角には、近衛邸跡地を整備した児童公園があり、小学生の娘が遊びに行く。そのすぐ南西が、一条邸跡である。どんぐりやふくろうのモチーフのついたブランコに乗る娘を見守りながら、ああ、このあたりで昭憲皇太后は入内までを過ごされたのだとあらためて思いを馳せる。明治天皇が幼いころを過ごされた中山邸跡も近衛邸跡の東側の並びにあり、両陛下がそれぞれ育たれた場はこれほど近かったのかと、その距離感に驚かされる。

御苑の砂利道を歩くと、一条邸跡の美しい大銀杏（おおいちょう）が目を引く。樹齢は不明だが、昭憲皇太后ももしやこの木を見ながら成長されたのだろうか、などと想像してみる。本書には、

故郷木

昔わが実をひろひにしふるさとのかしの大木はいまものこれり

　　　　　　　　　　　　　　　　　　　明治三十五年

　という一首が収められている。どんぐり拾いで親しんだ樫の木は当時からあったのかどうか。今まで何気なく通り過ぎてしまっていた場所であるが、昭憲皇太后の御歌をじっくり読んだあとに訪れると、思わず歩みが止まる。

　百七十年余り前に、この地で生を受けた女性。京都での日々が、昭憲皇太后の御人柄と感受性を育んだことに疑いはないだろう。京都を離れ東京へ移ったあとも、ここから望む山並みを思い、遠くこの生地を懐かしまれたであろうことがしみじみと思われる。屋敷の庭園跡に、昭憲皇太后の産湯に用いられたと伝えられる井戸「縣井（あがたい）」を今も見ることが出来る。井戸の横には、白い山茶花（さざんか）が花びらを落としていた。

　昭憲皇太后は誕生後、勝子（まさこ）と命名され、幼いころは富貴君（ふきぎみ）、のちに寿栄君（すえぎみ）と呼ばれた。九歳のときに母を、十四歳のときに父を病気でなくしている。皇后に内定し、入内の直前に美子皇后十八歳。明治天皇十六歳、美子皇后十八歳。ときに明治天皇十六歳、美子皇后十八歳。明治元年十二月二十八日に入内した。ときに明治天皇十六歳、美子皇后十八歳。子と改名。　明治元年十二月二十八日に入内した。

　大正三年（一九一四年）の崩御ののち、追号として昭憲皇太后が贈られた。明治天皇との間

にお子さまはなかった。

昭憲皇太后の父の一条忠香は、子どもたちの教育に熱心であった。幼いころから四書五経の素読、和学や漢籍を学ばせ、「物見の台」を設けて庶民の暮らしぶりへも目を向けさせたという。和歌の師は近衛忠熙であった。

本書にはとりあげられていないが、このような一首がある。

　　　　往時如夢

ねこの子をひざにおきつつふみよみし幼心もゆめとなりにき

　　　　　　　　　　　　　　　明治三十四年

なんとすてきな情景であろう。幼い日々、子猫を膝にのせて本を読む。猫のやわらかな毛と体温を感じながら、書物の世界に入り込み、まだ見ぬ世界への憧れをいだく。これから広がりゆく未来への心躍りを胸に、読書に没頭している少女。後年、「書を見るの楽しみより楽しみは無し」と語ったと伝えられるように、たいそうな読書好きで勉強家であったのだ。そん

な幼い日々も夢のように遠くなってしまったとの感慨が詠まれた、五十歳を過ぎてからの一首であるが、幼時のあたたかな手触りのある思い出が人生を照らすやさしさにつながっていることが感じられるのである。

読書言志

夜ひかる玉も何せむみをてらす書こそ人のたからなりけれ

明治十二年以前

光りかがやく宝石などよりも、書物こそが身を照らしてくれる宝なのだ、という。昭憲皇太后の、書物や学問への厚い信頼が感じられる。皇后となってから女子教育を熱心に奨励されたのも、学問によって世界がゆたかにひろがることを、身をもって感じておられたからであろう。

東京女子師範学校（現在のお茶の水女子大学）や華族女学校（現在の学習院女子中等科・高等科）を支援してたびたび行啓になり、それぞれの学校に御歌を下賜されている。それらの御歌には譜が付され、現在も校歌として歌い継がれている。

明治九年（一八七六年）二月に東京女子師範学校に贈られたのは、「みがかずば」という御歌である。

みがかずば玉も鏡も何かせむまなびの道もかくこそありけれ

宝石も鏡も、磨かなければ何にもなりません。学びの道というのも、まさにこのようなことです。自身をかがやかせるためには、研鑽（けんさん）を積んで自身を磨きつづけることです。

また、明治二十年三月には、華族女学校に「金剛石」「水は器」のふたつの御歌を下賜された。初めて発表になった時には、昭憲皇太后みずからが壇上で場内隅々にまで響きわたるような高いお声でお読みになったという。

　　金剛石

金剛石もみがかずば

珠のひかりはそはざらむ

　　Diamond

Even a diamond when not polished,

Beautiful light will not be refracted

34

人もまなびてのちにこそ
まことの徳はあらはるれ
時計のはりのたえまなく
めぐるがごとく時のまの
日かげをしみてはげみなば
いかなるわざかならざらむ

水は器

水はうつはにしたがひて
そのさまざまになりぬなり
人はまじはる友により
よきにあしきにうつるなり
おのれにまさるよき友を
えらびもとめてもろともに
こころの駒にむちうちて

People, as well, only after learning,
Gain true virtue
The hands on a timepiece rotate without pause,
As periods of time roll by
Working hard without wasting daylight
Leads to a splendid outcome

As Water Requires a Container

Adapting to containers,
Water becomes variously shaped
According to the friends one has,
One appears better or worse
Good friends who surpass me,
For those I seek to select
I will whip my mind as if it were a horse,

まなびの道にすすめかし

歌意としては、非常にわかりやすい。「金剛石」は、「みがかずば」と同様、つねに自分を高めるための努力を続ける必要性を説いている。また、「水は器」は、水が器によって形を変えるように、人は交わる友によって良くも悪くも変わるものであるから、自分に勝るよい人間を友として持ち、自らに厳しく学びの道をお進みなさいね、とあたたかく鼓舞するものである。

いずれも、ものごとの本質が象徴的に表され、説得力がある。どのように喩えれば年若い女子学生たちの心にひびくかということを、深く考えられた故の作であろう。それはまた、自身の心の内をしずかに見つめて導き出された、自戒をこめた言葉でもあった。

実際、「フランクリン十二徳の御歌」として知られる十二首のなかの、「勤労」と題された一首はこうである。

勤労

みがかずば玉の光はいでざらむ人のこころもかくこそあるらし

Industry

If left unpolished
the glow of precious stones
will not luster forth;
it must also be quite true
of these human hears of ours.

先に挙げた「みがかずば」の歌と引きくらべると、「玉、鏡」が「玉の光」に、「学びの道」が「人のこころ」に置き換わっているが、求めるところは同じ。つねに勤勉に努力して、自らを高めるべきであるという志である。　昭憲皇太后は、若くして即位した明治天皇に入内したため、皇太子妃を経ることなく皇后となっている。先の皇后のお仕事ぶりに学ぶという準備期間のないまま、いきなり皇后という立場に置かれた重責と孤独は、いかばかりであったか。お手本のないままに、新しい時代の皇后像を手探りで作り上げねばならなかったのである。

明治九年、侍講の元田永孚は、アメリカの独立宣言を起草したひとりであるベンジャミン・フランクリンが掲げた十二徳について、昭憲皇太后にご進講した。すなわち、「節制」「清潔」「勤労」……「公義」など、自らの品性を高めるべくフランクリンが具体的に挙げた十二の徳目をご紹介した。皇后はつねづね、激動の時代の皇后としてどのようにあるべきか、はかりしれないプレッシャーと闘いながら模索されていたであろう。そのようなとき、このフランクリンの十二徳に出会い、和歌に翻案されたのである。大和言葉に直すことは、十二徳の本質をあらためて自身の内に深くしずめ、腑に落ちて納得するための作業であったのだろうと思う。

これらの御歌は、のちに国定教科書にも掲載され、広く知られることとなった。十二首すべてが本書に収められている。

さて、当時の御歌所（おうたどころ）式の和歌では、『古今和歌集』に用例のある言葉以外は使ってはいけないという厳しい制約があった。新しい文化、文物が否応なく流れ込んでくる明治時代に生活しながら歌を詠もうとしたとき、これはなかなかに難しいことであったろう。

本書には、西洋から入ってきた新しい文物を題材とした、次のような歌が収められている。

あがたもりをさむる道も一すぢに告げまつるべき糸口やこれ

　　　　　　　　　　　　　明治十二年以前

散る波のいろの水にて花文字もかきながす世となりにけるかな

　　　　　　　　　　明治十九年

ともしびの光をかりて外国（とつくに）のしらぬ野山もみる世なりけり

　　　　　　　明治三十二年

　それぞれの歌には御題がついているが、何を詠ったものか、わかるだろうか。一首目は、「テレグラフ」。電報、電信、電信機など、当時の先進技術であった。実は、黒船で来航したペリーが開国を迫る際、電信機と電線を日本に持ち込んだそうである。日本で最初の電線が架設されたのは、明治二年（一八六九年）のこと。和歌のなかでは「電線」という言葉を使

うことはできず、「糸」と表現されているのが興味深い。二首目は「インキ」を詠っている

が、これも「いろの水」となっている。三首目は、「幻燈」を詠んでいる。外国の見たこと

もなかった野山の様子も幻燈機で見ることができる時代になったのだ、という感慨。二首目

の「世となりにけるかな」、三首目の「世なりけり」とあるように、時代の変化をさまざま

に感じて詠まれているのがヴィヴィッドに伝わる。

　　　親

おもかげを写しとどむるわざもなき世にうせたりしおやをこそおもへ

　　　　　　　　　　　　　　　　　　　　　　　　　　　明治三十六年

ここでいう「面影を写し留むる技」とは、「写真」のこと。面影を写して留めておける、

写真という技術がなかった時代に亡くなってしまった親を思うのであるよ、と詠まれている。

本書には収録されていないが、写真については次のような御歌もあり、印象深い。

　　　写真

たらちねの親のみかげものこらましこのうつしゑのある世なりせば

明治二十一年

写真

新衣いまだきなれぬわがすがたうつしとどむるかげぞやさしき

明治二十二年

「うつしゑ」は、もともとは「現実を写した絵、写実的な絵」という意味で使われていた歌言葉であるが、明治時代になると「写真」の意が定着していった。写真というもののある時代であったなら、親のお姿も残ったであろうに、と両親の写真のないことを嘆く。年若く失った両親への、哀惜の念である。二首目は、冒頭でふれた、大礼服にティアラを着けた肖像写真が撮影された折のもの。「新衣」とは洋装、「やさしき」は「恥ずかしき」の意である。まだ着慣れず見慣れない、自身のドレス姿へのとまどいが伝わる。

他にも、「汽車」「電話」「飛行機」「新聞紙」「香水」「洋学」「望遠鏡」「靴」「海外旅」「幼稚園」「男女同権といふことを」など、新しい文物を臆することなく題材にしている。これらの言葉は和歌のなかに直接詠みこむのではなく、御題として歌の前におかれている。それ

らをいかに大和言葉で表現しようかと工夫する作業も、ある意味楽しまれたのではないだろうか。

明治天皇の御製は約十万首、昭憲皇太后の御歌は約三万首とされる。ともにおどろくほど多作である。単純計算で一日に何首以上、などという試算がなされたりもするが、この数の力というものは、歌作にとって案外大事な要素である。

歌を多く作っているうちに、自分を開きやすくなるというのは、実作者として感じるところである。たくさんたくさん作るなかで、自身の「実感」が歌に表れやすくなる。また一方で、知らなかった自分というものが歌の上に現れてくる。相反することのように思われるこの両方が起こるのが、創作活動のふしぎで面白いところである。

昭憲皇太后は六十五年の生涯のうち、四十五年を明治天皇とともに過ごした。夫婦で歌を作ったからこそ、相乗効果が働き多くの歌が生まれたのだという推察も、あながち間違ってはいないだろう。和歌にはやはり、互いに呼び交わすものという側面があり、意識するしないにかかわらず、身近で歌を詠む人と何らかの形で呼応するものである。相手への思いも、自ずと歌の形となって表れる。

越路へみゆきましましけるころをりにふれて

大宮のうちにありてもあつき日をいかなる山か君はこゆらむ

明治十二年以前

On Occasion

On such a hot day
even inside the palace;
we are most concerned
over those mountains that
His Majesty is crossing.

木曽路に行幸ましましけるころ朝霧のたてるをみて

大宮のとばりもしめる朝ぎりに君がこゆらむ山ぢをぞおもふ

明治十三年

With morning fog
leaving even curtains damp
here in the palace,
we think of His Majesty
journeying on those mountain roads!

一首目は、越路へ御幸中の天皇を思って詠まれた御歌。宮中にあってもこれほど暑い日ですのに、君はどの山を越えていらっしゃるのでしょうか、と思いやる。歌のなかには「気にする」「案じる」「心配する」といった言葉はないが、英訳では的確に "we are most concerned" が挿入されている。「いかなる」にこめられた皇后の思いがこのように英訳することに、目を開かれる。二首目も行幸中の天皇を思っているが、こちらは日本語の「おもふ」のままに "think" としながら、末尾の "！" に感情がこもる。どちらの御歌にも、"inside the palace" "here in the palace" で待つ皇后の思いやりが見える。そこには留守居のさびしさもあろうが、こうやって歌にすることで、相手の存在を近く感じることができるのである。

44

日本語で書かれた和歌を英語に翻訳することの困難さを思うと、気が遠くなりそうである。そもそも詩歌とはもちろん意味だけから成っているのではなく、措辞の妙、押韻、語順、リズムなどが複合的に干渉しあって詩を構築するのであり、さらに言えば、あえて意味をもたせない言葉に詩情を宿らせることが重要になる場合もある。そのような和歌翻訳の難しさと翻訳の手順については、明治天皇の御製百首を英訳したハロルド・ライト氏の前著『敷島の道に架ける橋——英語で伝えたい明治天皇百首』（中央公論新社）の「ある翻訳者の物語」に詳しい。

明治天皇のある一首の御製について、一年以上にわたって取り組んだこともあるそうだ。

翻訳者のなかには、詩情を無視して意味だけを単調な文章に訳するタイプ、また逆に、韻律にこだわりすぎて訳するタイプの人がいるそうである。そのような間にあって、ライト氏は、「詩の翻訳というものは、ピンと張った綱を渡るサーカスの技のようなもの。つまり、左右どちらに振れても落ちてしまう」と述べている。まさにそのような緊張感のなか、翻訳がなされたのだろう。

明治天皇について詠まれた歌をもう少し見てみよう。

花

君がためをらむとすればくろかみの上にみだれてちるさくらかな

花

明治十三年

きみがためえらびてをりし一枝（ひとえだ）に思ひしよりは花のすくなき

明治二十五年

手をのばして、高い枝を折ろうとする。少し揺らしただけで、桜の花びらがはらはらと散ってしまう。君への思い、黒髪の上にふりかかる花びらが耽美的なまでに美しい。二首目は、君のためにとせっかく一枝を折ったのに、思ったほど花がついていなかった残念な気分。けれど、そんな花のまばらさもまた趣があるものだ。

昭憲皇太后の御歌としては、「みがかずば」や「金剛石」「水は器」など、道徳的、教訓的な歌が世に広まって目立っている。いわゆるハレの歌であり、それらはもちろん意義深いものである。と同時に、日常のあれこれを詠んだケの歌も多く、しみじみと趣深い。植物への

46

こまやかな目が向けられた御歌も、深い余韻を残す。

　　菫

老松のうつほとなれるうちにさへすみれ花さくふるさとのには

　　　　　　　　　　　　　　　　　　　　　　　　　　明治二十五年

老木に空いた洞の中にさえ、すみれの花が咲くふるさとの庭。このような細部にこそ、懐かしさや切なさは息づくのである。

　　鏡

するおきし鏡わすれてわがかげをたれかとおもふ時もありけり

　　　　　　　　　　　　　　　　　　　　　　明治二十一年

　　櫛

櫛のはにあまりし昔おもふかなすくなくなれる髪をときつつ

　　　　　　　　　　　　　　　　　　　明治四十四年

鏡に映りこんだ自分の姿を見て、これは誰だろうと一瞬わからないことがある。少なくなった髪を梳きながら、昔は櫛の歯をあふれるくらい豊かな髪だったのに、と思う。どちらも、大いに共感するシチュエーションである。自らの加齢を、これほど正直に明らかに詠まれるのかとおどろいてしまうほどだが、歌という器への安心感ゆえだろう。

やんごとなき方々は、近づきがたく遠い存在であるとつい思ってしまうものだが、歌は、世俗のいろいろを飛び越して、直に心へ近づくことのできる詩形である。

この春、昭憲皇太后の御歌百首が英訳版として世界へ羽ばたくことを喜び、多くの人の心に届くことを願う。

48

明治神宮

Meiji Jingu (located in Tokyo)
The spirits of Emperor Meiji and Empress Shoken are enshrined.

華族女学校行啓
明治18年(1885年)11月13日、華族女学校の開校式に臨まれ、わが国の
女子教育における華族女学校の果たすべき役割の大きさを諭された。
画家：跡見 泰

The Empress at the Peeress' School
The Empress attended the opening ceremony for the school on November 13, 1885, which brought attention to the important role to be played by the Peeress' School in the education of girls.　　Artist: Atomi Yutaka

赤十字総会行啓
明治35年(1902年)10月21日、上野公園での日本赤十字社の総会と創
立25周年記念祝典に臨まれた皇后。　　　　　　　画家：湯浅一郎

The Empress Attending the General Meeting of the Japanese
Red Cross Society
On October 21, 1902, the Empress attended the general meeting of the
Japanese Red Cross Society on the occasion of its 25th anniversary held
in Ueno park.　　　　　　　　　　　　　Arist: Yuasa Ichiro

初雁の御歌
赤坂仮皇居の庭を散歩される皇后。初雁の飛ぶのをご覧になり、越後
巡幸中の天皇を偲んで「初雁の御歌」を詠まれた。　画家：鏑木清方

The Empress Composing a Waka Poem
The painting portrays the beautiful Empress, walking through the gardens
of the Akasaka Palace as she thinks about the Emperor, who was away on a
regional visit.　　　　　　　　　　　　　　Artist: Kaburaki Kiyokata

昭憲皇太后百首

花＊ながらすきかへされて苗代（なはしろ）の水田（みづた）に浮ぶつぼすみれかな＊＊

春田

◇明治十二年（1879年）以前

＊花も一緒に
＊＊春、うす紫の花が咲く

Spring Rice Fields

Tilling up the soil
together with blooming flowers
to make rice beds,
left blossoms of violets
floating in flooded paddies.

Hana nagara
suki-kaesarete
nawashiro no
mizuta ni ukabu
tsubo-sumire kana

＊
東北巡幸のほど杜鵑といふことを

みちのくになきてゆきけむほととぎすことしは声のすくなかりけり

＊明治九年六月二日、東北巡幸にご出発、七月二十一日、海路還幸。

52

*Singing of Hototogisu on the Imperial Tour
of the Northlands*

They all must have flown
to Michinoku,* singing,
the *hototogisu*;**
only few of them are heard
here in the palace this year.

*Michinoku ni
nakite yukiken
hototogisu
kotoshi wa koe no
sukunakarikeri*

*Michinoku. The Emperor was traveling to Michinoku in the far
north of the island Honshu, or present day Aomori prefecture.
**hototogisu* (Cuculus poliocephalus or Lesser Cuckoo) is a bird
renown for its song in poetry.

草花盛

御馬（みうま）には何を*かふらむ秋の野の草はみ**ながら花さきにけり

◇明治十二年（1879年）以前

*何を飼料として与えるのであろうか
**残らず

54

Flourishing of Plants

What fodder for feed
to give to palace horses?
In fields of autumn,
every single plant we see
is now flowering in full bloom.

Mi-uma ni wa
nani wo kauran
aki no no no
kusa wa minagara
hana sakinikeri

＊
みがかずば玉も鏡も何かせむまなびの道もかくこそありけれ
＊＊

◇明治十二年（1879年）以前

＊東京女子師範学校（現在のお茶の水女子大学）が明治九年（一八七六年）二月に設立された際に下賜された御歌。その後、譜が付され現在も校歌として歌い継がれている。

＊＊何になろう、何にもならない

（十一－十二頁、三十四頁参照、挿入画参照）

56

If left unpolished
neither jewels nor mirrors
are worth anything;
this is also very true
of the path of learning.

Migakazuba
tama mo kagami mo
nanika sen
manabi no michi mo
kaku koso arikere

The poem was gifted to Tokyo Woman's Normal School(present-day Ochanomizu University)in February 1876, when the School was established. The poem was subsequentry put to music and is still sung today as the School's song.

(See pp. *11-12*, p. *33* and insert picture)

花の春もみぢの秋のさかづきもほどほどにこそくままほしけれ

節*
制

◇明治十二年（1879年）以前

＊明治天皇の侍講であった元田永孚は昭憲皇太后にベンジャミン・フランクリンの自伝の一部をご進講した際、フランクリンが十二徳（節制、清潔、勤労、沈黙、確志、誠実、温和、謙遜、順序、節倹、寧静、公義）を大切にしていた旨伝えたとされる。これをお聞きになって感銘を受けられた昭憲皇太后が、その十二徳のそれぞれについて和歌を詠まれたのがここに記された御歌である。また、明仁天皇（当時）は平成六年（一九九四年）米国を公式訪問された際、ホワイトハウスでの歓迎式典のご挨拶の中でこのエピソードをご披露されている。

＊＊昭憲皇太后は明治天皇がお飲みになり過ぎないよう、ご心配されて詠まれたもの。

58

Temperance[*]

With the flowers of spring^{* * *}
or with the leaves of autumn,
it is our desire
that those cups of *sake*
be served in moderation.^{* *}

Hana no haru
momiji no aki no
sakazuki mo
hodo-hodo ni koso
kuma mahoshikere

*This poen is influenced, according to the accepted anecdote: "The Empress Shoken had learned from her tutor Motoda Nagazane that Benjamin Franklin of the United Sates highly valued the following virtues: temperance, cleanliness, industry, silence, resolution, sincerity, moderation, humility, order, frugality, tranquility and justice."
This story was repeated by Emperor Akihito when speaking at the White House on an official visit to the US in 1994.
* *It has been said that the Empress was deeply concerned about the amount of *sake* her husband Emperor Meiji drank on a daily basis.
* * *Cherry blossom viewing and gathering to admire the autumn leaves were both considered times for excess drinking.

しろたへの衣のちりは払へどもうきは心のくもりなりけり

◇明治十二年（1879年）以前

＊五十八頁註参照

*Cleanliness**

Even through the dust
is brushed completely away
from our white garment,
what really distress us
are those clouds in our hearts.

*Shirotae no
koromo no chiri wa
harae domo
uki wa kokoro no
kumori narikeri*

*Refer to footnote (p. 59)

(See pp. 35-36)

みがかずば玉の光はいでざらむ人のこころもかくこそあるらし

勤労*

◇明治十二年（1879年）以前

*五十八頁註参照

（三十六－三十七頁参照）

62

Industry*

If left unpolished
the glow of precious stones
will not luster forth;
it must also be quite true
of these human hearts of ours.

> *Migakazuba*
> *tama no hikari wa*
> *idezaran*
> *hito no kokoro mo*
> *kaku koso arurashi*

* Refer to footnote (p. 59)

(See pp. *35-36*)

沈*黙

すぎたるは及ばざりけり*かりそめ*の言葉もあだにちらさざらなむ

◇明治十二年（1879年）以前

＊五十八頁註参照
＊＊論語よりの引用
＊＊＊ちょっとした言葉も無意味には散らさないでほしい

Silence*

"Going to excess
is as wrong as falling short"**
So we should not be
scattering useless words
in a trifling manner.

Sugitaru wa
oyobazarikeri
karisome no
kotoba mo ada ni
chirasazaranan

*Refer to footnote (p. 59)
**An expression taken from analects of Confucius.

確志＊

人ごころかからましかば白玉のまたまは火にもやかれざりけり

◇明治十二年（1879年）以前

＊五十八頁註参照
＊＊ダイヤモンド

*Resolution**

May these hearts of ours
be firm in resolution
as the white jewels;**
those pure stones will not burn
even when faced with fire.

Hito-gokoro
kakaramashikaba
shira-tama no
matama wa hi ni mo
yakarezarikeri

*Refer to footnote (p. 59)
**Diamonds

とりどりにつくるかざしの花もあれどにほふこころのうるはしきかな

◇明治十二年（1879年）以前

五十八頁註参照

Sincerity*

Colorful flowers
may well beautifully adorn
the hair of a woman,
but fragrance of sincerity
is the heart's real elegance.

*Toridori ni
tsukuru kazashi no
hana mo aredo
niou kokoro no
uruwashiki kana*

* Refer to footnote (p. 59)

みだるべきをりをばおきて花桜まづゑむ**ほどをならひてしがな

温*和

◇明治十二年（1879年）以前

* 五十八頁註参照
** 笑む、咲むの二つの意味が含まれている。

70

Moderation*

Let us just learn
that blossoms of cherry
will someday scatter
although they do start to bloom
with such smiles of joy.

Midaru beki
ori woba okite
hana-zakura
mazu emu** *hodo wo*
naraite shigana

*Refer to footnote (p. 59)
** *"emu"* (笑む 咲む) means both "smile" and "break out in blooming".

謙遜[*]

高山のかげをうつしてゆく水の低（ひき）きにつくを心ともがな

◇明治十二年（1879年）以前

[*]五十八頁註参照
（二十四頁参照）

Humility*

The lofty mountains
are carried in reflection
by flowing waters;
this seeking of humble levels
should be the aim of human hearts.

*Taka-yama no
kage wo utsushite
yuku mizu no
hikiki ni tsuku wo
kokoro to mogana*

*Refer to footnote (p. 59)

(See p. 22)

順*
序

◇明治十二年（1879年）以前

おくふかき道もきはめむものごとの本末{もとすえ}をだにたがへざりせば

*
五十八頁註参照

74

Order*

Although deep and dark
any path can be followed
only when we know,
as in all other things,
where to start and when to end.

> *Oku-fukaki*
> *michi mo kiwamen*
> *mono-goto no*
> *moto-sue wo dani*
> *tagaezari seba*

* Refer to footnote (p. 59)

節*倹

呉竹のほどよきふしをたがへずば末葉（うらば）の露（つゆ）もみだれざらまし

◇明治十二年（1879年）以前

＊五十八頁註参照
＊＊ほどよくして程度をこえなければ、後に苦しむこともなかろう。

Frugality*

Living modest lives
like the smooth joints of bamboo,
life will be as stable
as the dew that remains saved
for those younger outer leaves.

Kure-take no**
hodoyoki fushi wo
tagaezuba
uraba no tsuyu mo
midarezaramashi

* Refer to footnote (p. 59)

寧静*

いかさまに身はくだくともむらぎもの心はゆたにあるべかりけり

◇明治十二年（1879年）以前

*　五十八頁註参照
**　どのように苦労するとも
***　心にかかる枕詞
****　ゆったりと

Tranquility *

No matter how much
we may be overwhelmed
or exhausted,
we should always sustain
a full and tranquil heart.

*Ikasama ni
mi wa kudaku tomo
muragimo no
kokoro wa yutani
arubekarikeri*

*Refer to footnote (p. 59)

国民をすくはむ道も近きよりおし及ぼさむ遠きさかひに

◇明治十二年（1879年）以前

＊五十八頁註参照

Justice*

To save our people
the way we need to follow
should begin nearby
and then extend further
to reach our distant places.

Kuni-tami wo
sukuwan michi mo
chikaki yori
oshi-oyobosan
tōki sakai ni

* Refer to footnote (p. 59)

治民如治水

あさしとてせけば*あふるる川水のこころや民の心なるらむ

◇明治十二年（1879年）以前

*せきとめれば

82

People's Hearts*

Even if shallow
river waters do overflow
when they are dammed;
it is the hearts of such streams
that resemble hearts of people.

Asashi tote
sekeba afururu
kawa-mizu no
kokoro ya tami no
kokoro naruran

* It has been said by some scholars that this poem expresses the
Empress' concern over government repression.

越路＊へみゆきましましけるころ

◇明治十二年（1879年）以前

はつかりをまつとはなしにこの秋は越路のそらのながめられつつ

＊明治十一年秋、天皇が北陸地方へ巡幸の折、皇后が初雁の飛ぶのをご覧になり詠まれた御歌。

（挿入画参照）

84

On an Imperial Journey

As if waiting
for the first geese to arrive
this year in autumn,
we* keep gazing at the sky
over Koshi in the north.**

Hatsu-kari wo
matsu to wa nashi ni
kono aki wa
Koshiji no sora no
nagamerare tsu-tsu

* Although the Empress often uses no pronoun at all in most of
these poems, since the subject is understood, it seems appropriate to
use the "royal we" or "majestic plural" ("we" instead of "I") when
needed, in these translations.
** The Empress was thinking about the Emperor who was then
traveling in Koshiji in the distant north.

(See the insert picture)

越路へみゆきましましけるころ浜殿＊にて

君のますあたりやいづこしらくものたなびくかたにみゆる山のは

＊浜離宮

86

Viewing from the Hama Villa*

We anxiously wonder
where could His Majesty be
in his journey;
now that we view those mountains
afar amidst the floating clouds.

Kimi no masu
atari ya izuko
shira-kumo no
tanabiku kata ni
miyuru yama no ha

* Hama Rikyu is an Imperial Villa located in Tokyo.

越路へみゆきまししけるころをりにふれて

大宮のうちにありてもあつき日をいかなる山か君はこゆらむ

（四十三頁参照）

◇明治十二年（1879年）以前

On Occasion

On such a hot day
even inside the palace;
we are most concerned
over those mountains that
His Majesty is crossing.

Ōmiya no
uchi ni arite mo
atsuki hi wo
ikanaru yama ka
kimi wa koyuran

(See pp. *44-45*)

故郷

ふるさとにかへりてみればすむ人の手ぶりも時におくれけるかな

＊京都
＊＊ならわし、風習

◇明治十二年（1879年）以前

Old Home

Going home* again
we see people living there,
in our former town,
have fallen behind the times
in all ways that they behave.

Furusato ni
kaerite mireba
sumu hito no
teburi mo toki ni
okurekeru kana*

* Both Emperor Meiji and Empress Shoken, after they moved the
captial of Japan to Tokyo, refer to the old capital of Kyoto as
"furusato" (home town) in their poems.

テレグラフ

あ
が
た
も
り
＊
を
さ
む
る
道
も
一
す
ぢ
に
告
げ
ま
つ
る
べ
き
糸
口
や
こ
れ

◇明治十二年（1879年）以前

＊地方を治める長

（十五－十六頁、三十九頁参照）

92

*Telegraph**

How do heads of regions
now report to the central office,
the ways they govern?
The clue is in just one thing:
a single thread of wire.

*Agata-mori
osamuru michi mo
hito-suji ni
tsuge matsuru beki
ito-guchi ya kore*

*Telegraph was an advanced technology of that period.

(See p. *15*, p. *38-40*)

靴

とのもりのくつの音（ね）たかくきこゆなり御垣（みかき）の月も影ふけぬらむ

◇明治十二年（1879年）以前

Boots

We can clearly hear
sounds of the boot steps
of Imperial guards;
the moonlight on our palace walls
must also glow at this late hour.

Tono-mori no
kutsu no ne takaku
kikoyu nari
mikaki no tsuki mo
kage fukenuran

花

君がためをらむとすればくろかみの上にみだれてちるさくらかな

◇明治十三年（1880年）

（十三-十四頁、四十六頁参照）

Cherry Blossoms

Breaking off a branch
of the blooming cherry
for His Majesty,
petals of flowers are scattered
over our long black locks.

*Kimi ga tame
oran to sureba
kuro-kami no
ue ni midarete
chiru sakura kana*

(See p. *13*, p. *47*)

折にふれて

すだく蚊のこゑいぶせしとおぼすらむのきばをぐらきかりの宮居に

◇明治十三年（1880年）

*集まってくる蚊を不愉快と思うであろう。
**地方に行幸の際の仮の居所

On Occasion

It must be awful
for His Majesty to hear
swarms of mosquitoes
under the gloomy eaves
of the provisional palace.*

Sudaku ka no
koe ibuseshi to
obosuran
nokiba oguraki
kari no miya-i ni

---

*Provisional palace: Temporary dwellings of the Emperor when he
was traveling outside of the capital.

月

かりそめの露のうへにもやどるらむ植木の市の秋の夜の月

◇明治十三年（1880年）

Moon

Now a tiny moon
must have also come to dwell
in the fleeting dew
resting on a potted plant
in the autumn night market.

Karisome no
tsuyu no ue ni mo
yadoruran
ueki no ichi no
aki no yo no tsuki

◇明治十三年（1880年）

木曽路に行幸ましましけるころ朝霧のたてるをみて

大宮のとばりもしめる朝ぎりに君がこゆらむ山ぢをぞおもふ
*

＊室内をへだてるたれ幕
（四十三―四十四頁参照）

*Seeing Morning Fog while His Majesty is
Traveling to Kisoji**

With morning fog
leaving even curtains damp
here in the palace,
we think of His Majesty*
journeying on those mountain roads!

*Ōmiya no
tobari mo shimeru
asa-giri ni
kimi ga koyuran
yama-ji wo zo omou*

＊Kisoji: Mountainous road joining Tokyo and Kyoto, also called
Nakasendo.

(See p. 45)

恋筆

思ふことかきつくしてむとる筆のその命毛のあらむかぎりは

◇明治十三年（1880年）

＊「てむ」は意志を表す。
＊＊筆の穂先の毛。「命ある限り」との掛けことば

Love

We shall fully write
with all the deepest feelings
in this heart of ours
as long as this writing brush
still keeps its lively tip!*

Omou koto
kaki-tsukushiten
toru fude no
sono inochi-ge no
aran kagiri wa

*Lively tip: the original Japanese word "命毛"(*inochi-ge*) which literally means "the life bristle of a writing brush", is the tip of a brush, being the most important part of the brush when writing. Here, the Empress seems to play on words, as she often does, by expressing "as long as the brush is kept in good shape" but also suggesting "as long as she lives".

◇明治十四年（1881年）

二月二十一日八王子の御猟場よりかへらせたまひける日
狩場雪といふことをよませたまひけるに

うさぎとるあみにも雪のかかる日にぬれしみけしを*おもひこそやれ

106

*On His Majesty Returning in the Snow
from a Hunting Trip to Hachioji**

On a day like this
when nets for catching rabbits
are covered with snow,
we are quite concerened over
His Majesty in wet clothing!

*Usagi toru
ami ni mo yuki no
kakaru hi ni
nureshi mikeshi wo
omoi koso yare*

* Hachioji was at the time an open mountainous area west of Tokyo.
Emperor Meiji did enjoy horseback riding and hunting rabbits
apparently in the rainy snow.

雁

いかりおろすみなとのなみに月ふけてふねのうへちかくわたるかりがね

◇明治十四年（1881年）

Wild Geese

Once the anchor dropped,
harbor waves kept rolling in
with the late night moon;
then just over the regal ship
the passing of wild geese.

Ikari orosu
minato no nami ni
tsuki fukete
fune no ue chikaku
wataru karigane

北海道にみゆきましましけるころ

◇明治十四年（1881年）

＊
宮城野（みやぎの）のはぎのさかりを見ましてもみその秋をおぼしいづらむ

＊仙台の東部。萩の名所

110

On a Journey to Hokkaido

Viewing bush clover
in full bloom in Miyagino*
must be bringing back
memories for His Majesty
of the palace autumn garden.

*Miyagino no
hagi no sakari wo
mimashite mo
mi-sono no aki wo
oboshi-izuran*

*Miyagino is an area to the east of the present city of Sendai in
Miyagi prefecture, known for its field of bush clover. As His Majesty
was passing by Miyagino on his way to Hokkaido, the Empress who
stayed at the palace in Tokyo, was imagining the places His Majesty
was visiting.

冬人事

みこしぢの雪にこもりてをとめらは夏の衣や織りいだすらむ

◇明治十四年（1881年）

＊越前、越中、越後（現在の福井・富山・新潟）

112

People in Winter

Once snowbound at home
young women of Mikoshiji*
must be now at work
making clothing for summer
by weaving on their looms.

Mikoshiji no
yuki ni komorite
otome-ra wa
natsu no koromo ya
ori-idasuran

*Mikoshi or Koshi are two old names of the region that runs along
the Japan Sea coast in Hokuriku, or "snow country" area of Japan. At
the end of 7th century, Koshi was divided into three separate
provinces: Echizen, Etchu and Echigo.

梅
の
は
な
ふ
ふ
み
し
ほ
ど
に
く
ら
ぶ
れ
ば
く
れ
な
ゐ
う
す
く
な
り
に
け
る
か
な

紅梅

◇明治十五年（1882年）

＊つぼみのころ

114

Red Blossom Plum Tree

Blooms of flowering plum
when compared to the time
they were still in bud,
have become somewhat paler
in their color of crimson.

Ume no hana
fufumishi hodo ni
kurabureba
kurenai usuku
narinikeru kana

向が岡にみゆきましましける夜雨いみじうふりいでければ

◇明治十六年（1883年）

みくるまを待つまひさしき夕やみにむねとどろかす雨のおとかな

（二十二頁参照）

His Majesty's Travel in the Rain

Waiting so long
for His Majesty's carriage
here at nightfall,
this heart of ours is throbbing
to the sounds of the rain.

Mi-kuruma wo
matsu ma hisashiki
yūyami ni
mune todorokasu
ame no oto kana

(See pp. *20-21*)

花

たらちねの[＊]いまもいまさば大御代のさかりの花もみせましものを

◇明治十七年（1884年）

＊親。両親。父母。

118

＊
たらちねのいまもいまさば大御代のさかりの花もみせましものを

花

◇明治十七年（1884年）

＊親。両親。父母。

118

Cherry Blossoms

Were he still with us
the dear father* of ours,
we would have him view
cherry blossoms in full bloom
and the flowering of the realm.

> *Tarachine* no*
> *ima mo imasaba*
> *ō-mi-yo no*
> *sakari no hana mo*
> *misemashi mono wo*

* "*Tarachine*" could mean 1)mother 2)parents 3)father. In this case, for various reasons, it seems to be the father of the Empress, Ichijō Tadaka (1812-1863)

歳暮

＊
しろしめす大御国内にことなくてくるる年こそのどけかりけれ

◇明治十七年（1884年）

＊お治めになる

（十六－十七頁）

120

End of the Year

The whole country
under His Majesty's reign
has remained at peace;
and, indeed, the end of this year
is truly calm and tranquil.

Shiroshimesu
ō-mi-kunuchi ni
koto nakute
kururu toshi koso
nodokekarikere

(See p. *16*)

歳暮

大宮のみ簾[す]ものこらずかけかへていそぐににたる年のくれかな

◇明治十七年（1884年）

End of the Year

Now we have replaced
all of our bamboo blinds
here in the palace,
we seem to be hurrying
as the year comes to an end.

Ōmiya no
misu mo nokorazu
kake-kaete
isogu ni nitaru
toshi no kure kana

◇明治十八年（1885年）

西の海へみゆきましましけるころ船中夏月といふことを

おほきみのみふねすずしく照*すらむ明石の浦の夏の夜の月

＊清らかで澄んでいる。曇りがない。

124

*On the Emperor's Journey to Western Japan
and Viewing the Moon on a Summer Night*

His Majesty's ship
must be clearly all aglow
in such moonlight
as they sail the Akashi* coast
on a night of summer moon.

*Ōkimi no
mi-fune suzushiku
terasuran
Akashi no ura no
natsu no yo no tsuki*

*Akashi is a beautiful stretch of shore on the Inland Sea near the
present city of Kobe.

夕立

摘みのこす桑の林にかぜたちて夕立すなり富岡＊のさと

◇明治十八年（1885年）

＊群馬県富岡市。養蚕業がさかんで、富岡製糸場がある。

Evening Shower

We were still picking
leaves in a mulberry grove
when quickly the wind
of a sudden summer shower
struck Tomioka* village.

Tsumi-nokosu
kuwa no hayashi ni
kaze tachite
yūdachi sunari
Tomioka no sato*

*The Tomioka area in Gumma Prefecture, known for silk mills, is a mountainous area north of Tokyo. Mulberry groves are grown all over the area to provide the leaves, the food of silkworms. Traditionally the leaves were hand picked daily.

月

たらちねの袖にすがりて見しかげも思ひぞいづる秋の夜の月[*]

◇明治十八年（一八八五年）

[*]百十八頁参照。

Moon

How we now recall
clinging to our mother's sleeve
as we viewed the moon.
Oh, those nights of autmn
with the moonlight all aglow.

Tarachine no
sode ni sugarite
mishi kage mo
omoi zo izuru
aki no yo no tsuki

故郷苅萱

昔わが野をうらやみてうゑおきしかるかやいかにしげりあふらむ
*

◇明治十九年（1886年）

*苅茅。イネ科の多年草

130

Pampas Grass at Our Home

A long time ago
we, longing for natural fields,
planted pampas grass;
now it must grow in profusion
in the garden at our home.

Mukashi waga
no wo urayamite
ue-okishi
karukaya ikani
shigeriauran

月

大宮のみはしの月にきこゆなり四谷あたりのをぐるまの音

◇明治十九年（1886年）

Moon

As we view the moon
on the steps of our palace
we can hear the sounds
of carriages passing by
the area of Yotsuya. *

*Ōmiya no
mi-hashi no tsuki ni
kikoyu nari
Yotsuya atari no
oguruma no oto*

* Yotsuya is an area in Tokyo, far enough from the palace.

観菊会

秋ごとにつらなる人の数そひてうたげにぎはふ菊のはなぞの
*

◇明治十九年（1886年）

＊参会者が多くなる。　毎年秋赤坂離宮で観菊会が催された。

（十三頁参照）

134

Viewing Chrysanthemums

Every autumn now,
our invited guests of state
have grown in number;
we have a bustling banquet
in the chrysanthemum garden.

Aki goto ni
tsuranaru hito no
kazu soite
utage nigiwau
kiku no hana-zono

(See pp. *12-13*)

インキ

散る波のいろの水にて花文字もかきながす世となりにけるかな

（三十九頁参照）

◇明治十九年（1886年）

Ink

Using water
in colors of splashing waves
we write fluidly
in florid calligraphy;
such is our world today.

Chiru nami no
iro no mizu nite
hana-moji mo
kaki-nagasu yo to
narinikeru kana

(See pp. 38-39)

香水

すずしくもかをれる水やそそがまし解き洗ひたるくろかみの上に *

* さわやかである

◇明治二十年（1887年）

Perfume

Wouldn't it be
so refreshing to have
perfumed water
poured over these black tresses,
once all undone and washed?

*Suzushiku mo
kaoreru mizu ya
sosogamashi
toki araitaru
kuro-kami no ue ni*

鏡

すゑおきし鏡わすれてわがかげをたれかとおもふ時もありけり

◇明治二十一年（１８８８年）

（四十七頁参照）

Mirror

Having forgotten
our mirror had been placed there,
it happened that
we wondered who the person was
when viewing our own reflection.

Sue-okishi
kagami wasurete
waga kage wo
tareka to omou
toki mo arikeri

(See p. 50)

洋学

石の筆とるおとすなり外国（とつくに）の文字のつづりをたれ学ぶらむ

◇明治二十一年（1888年）

＊

＊石筆。やわらかいろう石で作った筆。石盤に書く。

142

Western Learning

We hear sounds coming
from those "stone writing brushes"; *
someone must be learning
spelling in another language
used in foreign lands abroad.

Ishi no fude
toru oto sunari
totsu-kuni no
moji no tsuzuri wo
tare manaburan

* stone writing brush: A pencil made of soft stone used for writing
on a slate board.

洋学

横文字をまなばざる身はをさなごがよみたがへるもしらぬなりけり

◇明治二十二年（1889年）

144

Western Learning

If we ourselves
do not study western writings,
we will never know
if our young children ever
make a mistake in reading.

*Yokomoji wo
manabazaru mi wa
osanago ga
yomi-tagaeru mo
shiranunarikeri*

若菜

春雨のちりをあらひし初若菜ぬれてもつまむ君がおもの*に

◇明治二十三年（1890年）

＊召し上がりもの。御食事

Spring Greens

The first young greens
washed by the rain of spring...
depite of being wet,
we still go forth to pick them
for His Majesty to saver.

Harusame no
chiri wo araishi
hatsu-wakana
nurete mo tsuman
kimi ga omono ni

わが君はきこしめさずやほととぎすみはしに近きいまのひとこゑ

杜鵑

◇明治二十三年（1890年）

Hototogisu*

His Majesty
did he not hear it at all?
the *hototogisu*?
so very near the palace stairs,
just now a single song!

Waga kimi wa
kikoshimesazu ya
hototogisu
mi-hashi ni chikaki
ima no hito-koe

* *hototogisu*: Refer to footnote (p. 53)

のりもののうちにさくらのちりくるを

吉野山みささぎ＊近くなりぬらむちりくる花もうちしめりたる

＊後醍醐天皇の塔尾御陵。吉野山にある

◇明治二十三年（1890年）

◇1890 (Meiji23)

*On Cherry Blossom Falling into our
Carriage*

On mount Yoshino
we seem to be approaching
the Imperial Tomb;*
even falling cherry flowers
are now tinged with sorrow.

*Yoshino-yama
misasagi chikaku
narinuran
chiri-kuru hana mo
uchi-shimeritaru*

*The mausoleum of Emperor Godaigo, the 96th Emperor of Japan,
who founded the capital during his reign in Yoshino.

151

風をいたみ鴨はたちにし水錆江に上毛ばかりぞちり浮びたる

冬江

みさびえ
うはげ

◇明治二十三年（1890年）

＊風は激しいので
＊＊たまり水のにごった入江

（二十頁参照）

Winter Bay

As strong winds blew
all the ducks just flew away
from murky waters,
leaving nothing there at all
but scattered floating feathers.

Kaze wo itami
kamo wa tachinishi
misabie ni
uwage bakari zo
chiriukabitaru

(See pp. *18-19*)

車中見山

ふるさとの西の都はくるまより見わたすかぎり山にぞありける

◇明治二十三年（1890年）

154

Viewing Mountains from Carriage

Seen from a carriage
this capital of the West,*
our old hometown,
is nothing but mountains
just as far as one can see!

Furuasato * *no*
nishi no miyako wa
kuruma yori
miwatasu kagiri
yama ni zo arikeru

* *"Furusato"*(hometown) and *"Nishi no Miyako"*(Capital of the West)
are the terms the Empress uses to refer to the old capital of Kyoto.
Tokyo is, of course, the new Eastern Capital.

社頭祈世

神風の伊勢の内外のみやばしらゆるぎなき世をなほいのるかな

◇明治二十四年（1891年）

＊
「伊勢」の枕詞。内宮外宮の宮柱のゆるぎないごとく、ゆるぎない世を祈る。

（十九頁参照）

Violets

Even hollow places
in trunks of ancient pine trees
are growing clumps
of violet in the gardens
of our home of long ago.

Oi-matsu no
utsuho to nareru
uchi ni sae
sumire hana saku
furusato* no niwa

*furusato: Refer to footnote (P. 155)

(See p. *49*)

花

きみがためえらびてをりし一枝（ひとえだ）に思ひしよりは花のすくなき

◇明治二十五年（1892年）

（四十六頁参照）

Cherry blossoms

Selecting a small branch
to present to His Majesty,
and breaking it off,
we could see, then, the blooms
were fewer than we believed.

Kimi ga tame
erabite orishi
hito eda ni
omoishi yori wa
hana no sukunaki

(See p. *48*)

烏

あらそひてねぐらしめけむ＊もみぢやま烏_{からす}のはねのおほくちりたる

◇明治二十五年（1892年）

＊皇居の中の場所

162

Crows

After the squabble
crows must have seized the roost
at Momijiyama;*
many of their feathers
are still scattered all about.

> *Arasoite*
> *negura shimeken*
> *Momijiyama*
> *karasu no hane no*
> *ōku chiritaru*

* Momijiyama: An area within the palace grounds.

石筆*

書く文字のつたなきあともとどまらぬ石の筆こそうれしかりけれ

◇明治二十五年（1892年）

*百四十二頁註参照

（十五頁参照）

164

Slate Pencils *

Even if we wrote
something in an unskilled hand
it could be erased;
oh, these "stone writing brushes"
bring us joy of easiness.

Kaku moji no
tsutanaki ato mo
todomaranu
ishi no fude koso
ureshikarikere

＊ Slate pencils: Apparently, she was referring to writing on those
individual "black boards" called "slates" that were popular in Western
schools at that time. Writing was done with "slate pencils".

(See pp. *14-15*)

夏井

山城＊のみやこに残る祐＊＊の井の水は夏さへつめたかりけり

＊平安京、京都
＊＊明治天皇産湯の井戸。京都御苑内に残っている。

◇明治二十七年（1894年）

166

Summer Well

In Yamashiro,*
the former capital,
there remains a well
named "Sachi" where water is
always cold even in summer.

*Yamashiro no
miyako ni nokoru
Sachi no i no
mizu wa natsu sae
tsumetakarikeri*

＊Yamashiro refers to the area around Kyoto, the former capital. The well's name "Sachi", the Emperor's childhood name means 'good fortune'; and that well still exists in the Kyoto Palace Garden.

雁

広島の行宮*さしていそぐらむはるけき空をわたるかりがね

◇明治二十七年（1894年）

*この年九月、大本営が広島に置かれた。

168

Wild Geese

Appearing to fly
to the Imperial Headquarters*
in Hiroshima,
passing geese are hastening
through a very distant sky.

*Hiroshima no
kari-miya* sashite
isoguran
harukeki sora wo
wataru karigane*

Kari-miya (temporary palace) indicates the Emperor's temporary
headquarters in Hiroshima. The Emperor moved there so that he
could be closer to the military activities during the war with China.

連日雨

*
ことそぎし宮居いかにとおもふかなきのふもけふも雨ごもりして

＊諸事質素を旨とした

◇1894 (Meiji27)

Raining Everyday

Living so humbly
at the "temporary palace",*
His Majesty concerns us
by being closed in with rain
both yesterday and today.

*Kotosogishi
miya-i ikani to
omou kana
kinō mo kyō mo
ama-gomori shite*

* Temporary palace: refer to footnote (p. 169)

撫子露

それ[*]ながらささげむとおもふ撫子の露はをる手にこぼれけるかな

◇明治二十九年（1896年）

＊露のついたまま

172

Dew on Pinks

We wished to offer
His Majesty these flowering pinks
just as they were
covered with dew, but when picked
those drops trickled over our hands.

Sorenagara
sasagen to omou
nadeshiko no
tsuyu wa oru te ni
koborekeru kana

秋風

ひとかたに萩もすすきもなびくなり野をつくしてや風のふくらむ

◇明治二十九年（1896年）

Autumn Breeze

In their bending
bush clover and pampas grass
all tilt the same way;
a brisk wind must be blowing
strongly over all the fields.

Hito-kata ni
hagi mo susuki mo
nabiku nari
no wo tsukushite ya
kaze no fukuran

社頭冬月

みたらしも柄杓ながらにこほる夜の月かげさむし神の広前

＊御手洗。神仏を拝む前に参拝者が手や口を洗い清める所

◇明治二十九年（1896年）

176

Winter Moon at the Shrine

The purifying water
together with its dipper
are all frozen tonight
under the cold moonlight
there in front of the deities.

Mitarashi mo
hisaku nagara ni
kōru yo no
tsuki-kage samushi
kami no hiromae

一月三十日の夜月前神楽といふことを

霜さゆる夜はのみかぐら月の輪のみささぎまでもきこえあぐらむ*

◇明治二十九年（1896年）

*京都市東山区泉山にある孝明天皇の御陵

178

Mikagura* under the Moon on 30th Day
of the First Month

In brightness of frost
the sacred music at night
surely must be heard
as far as Tsukinowa**
the Imperial Mausoleum.

Shimo sayuru
yowa no mikagura
Tsukinowa no
misasagi made mo
kikoe-aguran

* *Mikagura*: the sacred music played for the deities
* *Tsukinowa: the mausoleum of Emperor Komei

英照皇太后の崩御ましましけるころ

◇明治三十年（1897年）

神あがりましぬときくはまことかといひもあへぬになみだこぼるる

＊孝明天皇の女御。この年一月十一日に崩御。
＊＊崩御する
＊＊＊十分に言いおえることができないのに

Death of Empress Dowager Eisho *

When we had heard
of her passing in spirit
we did not finish
asking "Is it really true?"
Yet tear drops flowed from our eyes.

Kamu agari
mashinu to kiku wa
makoto ka to
iimo aenu ni
namida koboruru

* Empress Dowager Eisho : Empress consort of Emperor Komei,
father of Emperor Meiji.

英照皇太后の崩御ましましけるころ

したしくものたまひにけるみことばをおもひいではなみだぐみつつ

◇明治三十年（１８９７年）

Death of Empress Dowager Eisho *

When we recall
those kind words she said to us
with deep affection,
it is such loving memories
that always fill our eyes with tears.

Shitashiku mo
notamainikeru
mi-kotoba wo
omoi-idete wa
namida-gumi tsu-tsu

*Empress Dowager Eisho: Refer to footnote (p. 181)

英照皇太后の崩御ましましけるころ

◇明治三十年（1897年）

たまぐしにかかるなみだの露ながら手向けてもなほゆめかとぞおもふ

Death of Empress Dowager Eisho *

We proffered up a branch
of the sacred *sakaki* tree * *
damp with dew of tears;
yet we were still wondering
if it were merely a dream.

Tamagushi ni
kakaru namida no
tsuyu nagara
tamukete mo nao
yume ka to zo omou

* Empress Dowager Eisho: Refer to footnote (p. 181)
* * A Shinto ritual to offer up a branch of the sacred tree to a deity
or the soul of the deceased.

奈良県より人の松虫を奉りければ

籠のうちのあまたのこゑにみその＊ふのむしはきこえぬ時もありけり

＊御苑

186

*On the Offering of Bell Crickets by a Person
from Nara*

Due to the singing
coming from all the cages,*
there were occasions
when we could no longer hear
insects in the palace garden.

*Ko no uchi no
amata no koe ni
mi-sonou no
mushi wa kikoenu
toki mo arikeri*

*Keeping singing insects in cages has been a popular hobby in Japan.

いかばかりうれしかるらむゆるされてみかはの水を小田にひく日は

五月二十二日みその*のながれかれがれになりたるをいかでといぶかりしに苗代にひきたるなりとのたまはせければ

◇明治三十年（1897年）

＊京都御所の中の流れ。御所の御溝水はもと鞍馬口から相国寺内を流れて御苑内に入っていたので、苗代時には田の用水にひかれることもあったという。

（十七－十八頁参照）

188

Water on the 22nd of May

How happy they must be
the day when farmers are allowed
to draw in water*
from the stream in the palace grounds
to flood their own fields of rice.

> *Ikabakari*
> *ureshikaruran*
> *yurusarete*
> *mi-kawa no mizu wo*
> *oda ni hiku hi wa*

*In the season of planting rice, farmers were permitted to draw
water from the upper reaches of the stream that was flowing through
the palace grounds in Kyoto.

(See pp. *16-17*)

月さやかなりける夜

たちばなにさくらにかげのさしわたるくもまの月のなつかしきかな

◇明治三十年（1897年）

＊紫宸殿の前庭には、東の左近の桜、西の右近の橘がある。

190

Night of a Bright Moon

It is the bright moon
passing between the clouds
and shedding it's clear light
over the wild orange and cherry trees
that we keep as fond memories.

Tachibana ni
sakura ni kage no
sashi-wataru
kumo-ma no tsuki no
natsukashiki kana

✴ In front of the main hall of the old Imperial Palace in Kyoto, there stand the traditional *tachibana* (a wild orange) on the West and the cherry tree on the East. Both can be seen today.
Her own childhood home was nearby: she must have seen the scene often.

朝市

雨はれし朝(あした)の市にひさぐ＊菜のぬれたるいろのきよげなるかな

◇明治三十一年（1898年）

＊商いをする

Morning Market

Once the rain cleared,
all vegetables being sold
in the morning market
have freshly picked colors
in the lingering wetness.

Ame hareshi
ashita no ichi ni
hisagu na no
nuretaru iro no
kiyogenaru kana

往事

この宮に年をかさねておもふかなとほき東といひし昔を

◇明治三十一年（1898年）

＊東京の御所

194

The Past

Now that we have lived
many years in this palace,
we still recall
we used to speak of this place,
long ago, as the "distant East".*

Kono miya ni
toshi wo kasanete
omou kana
tōki azuma to
iishi mukashi wo

* After Emperor Meiji was enthroned, the capital was moved from
Kyoto to Tokyo.

往事

大御代にか*へるはじめのみいくさもいまはむかしのゆめとなりにき

◇明治三十一年（1898年）

*明治維新のころに行われた王政復古のための戦争

The Past

Even those battles*
that brought the Restoration
of Imperial Reign,
have become for us today
mere dreams of a distant past.

*Ō-mi-yo ni
kaeru hajime no
mi-ikusa mo
ima wa mukashi no
yume to nariniki*

* The civil war between the government and the southern samurai clans.

197

幻燈

ともしびの光をかりて外国のしらぬ野山もみる世なりけり

（三十九頁参照）

◇明治三十二年（1899年）

Magic Lantern

By using the light
of just the flame of a lamp
we view fields and mountains
of lands never seen before.
This is our world of today.

Tomoshibi no
hikari wo karite
totsu-kuni no
shiranu no-yama mo
miru yo narikeri

(See p. *39*)

うれしきもの

いかにやとおもひしことをいひいでてうち泣くばかりよろこばれたる

◇明治三十二年（1899年）

Joyful Things

It gives us great joy
to finally say something
we had been thinking
which makes others so happy
that they shed tears of joy.

Ikani ya to
omoishi koto wo
ii-idete
uchi-naku bakari
yorokobaretaru

うれしきもの

たび衣かへりてみればみこたちの車やどりにいでむかへたる

◇明治三十二年（1899年）

Joyful Things

It's joyful to see
children at the carriage house
waiting to greet us
on our return to the palace
from an Imperial journey.

Tabi-goromo
kaerite mireba
mi-ko tachi no
kuruma-yadori ni
ide-mukaetaru

振天府*

いのちにもかへし品品あつめます大御ごころのうちをこそ思へ

◇明治三十三年（1900年）

*皇居内桜田門の近くの土手の上にある。日清戦争後、陸海軍将兵の功を伝えるため戦死者の写真、名簿などをおさめた。

204

Museum of War*

In exchange for lives
these various items of war
have been gathered here;
do think upon the feelings
deep inside His Majesty's heart.

Inochi ni mo
kaeshi shina-jina
atsumemasu
ō-mi-gokoro no
uchi wo koso omoe

* It is located within the palace grounds. After the Sino-Japanese
War, in order to pay tribute to the brave deeds of the soldiers, it was
decided to gather there various memorial items such as photos and
soldiers' name lists.

思往事

庭ながら大内山_*をあふぎ見し里居_{**}のむかしおもひいでつつ

*皇居
**実家にいたころ。皇太后の実家一条家は京都御所近くにあった。

◇明治三十三年（1900年）

Recalling the Past

From our own garden
we would view with deep respect
the Imperial palace;
memories of our native home*
do just keep returning.

*Niwa nagara
ō-uchiyama wo
augi-mishi
sato-i no mukashi
omoi-ide tsu-tsu*

*The Empress' old home was located adjacent to the palace, in the
present day Kyoto Palace Garden.

寝覚月

とのゐ人ねしづまりたるさ夜なかにひとりおきいでて月をみるかな

*

◇明治三十四年（1901年）

＊宿直の人

Moon

When our attendants
have all gone soundly asleep
in depth of the night,
we wake up all alone
and just gaze at the moon.

Tonoi-bito
ne-shizumaritaru
sa-yonaka ni
hitori oki-ide te
tsuki wo miru kana

述懐

あふことのまれなる御代にあひながら昔をしのぶをりもありけり

◇明治三十四年（1901年）

Recollections

Though we are living
under most exceptional reign,
yet from time to time
we recall our memories
of our lives of long ago.

Aukoto no
marenaru mi-yo ni
ainagara
mukashi wo shinobu
ori mo arikeri

霧

かりみやのありともみえず代々幡*のさとの杉むらきりこめてけり

_{よはた}

◇明治三十五年（1902年）

*代々木・幡ヶ谷を合わせて代々幡といった。今の明治神宮の地は代々木御料地で、ここに行幸啓のための小休憩所があった。かりみやはそれをさす。

◇1902 (Meiji35)

Fog

We can't even see
the royal lodge itself*
in the ceder wood
with the fog now covering
the village of Yoyohata.**

*Kari-miya no
ari to mo miezu
Yoyohata no
sato no sugi-mura
kiri kometekeri*

Karimiya (Temporary palace) refers to a rest lodge the Emperor
had constructed in the Yoyogi area which had the old name of
Yoyohata.** It is the area where Meiji Jingu Shrine stands today.

故郷木

昔わが実をひろひにしふるさとのかしの大木（おほき）はいまものこれり

◇明治三十五年（1902年）

（三十‐三十一頁参照）

Old Hometown Tree

Long, long ago
we would gather acorns
in the old hometown;*
even today it still stands
the gigantic oak tree.

*Mukashi waga
mi wo hiroinishi
furusato no
kashi no ōki wa
ima mo nokoreri*

*Hometown: The Empress was born and raised in Kyoto.

(See pp. *28-29*)

書[*]

さくら木にいまだのぼせぬいにしへの書（ふみ）の巻（まき）こそたからなりけれ

◇明治三十五年（1902年）

Writings

Scrolls of ancient words
existing before printing
on those cherry blocks,*
are writings that, indeed,
are now considered treasures.

Sakura-gi ni
imada nobosenu
inishie no
fumi no maki koso
takara narikere

*Cherry trees were used to make printing blocks.

机

大臣《おとど》よりささげしふみのおほきかな大み机の上せばきまで

◇明治三十五年（1902年）

218

Desk

Written documents
submitted by officials
are so numerous
they would barely fit at all
on His Majesty's grand desk.

Otodo yori
sasageshi fumi no
ōki kana
ō-mi-tsukue no
ue sebaki made

親

おもかげを写*しとどむるわざもなき世にうせたりしおやをこそおもへ

◇明治三十六年（1903年）

＊写真技術のなかった

（四十頁参照）

Parents

They lived in an age
when we could not keep
images of them;
so we should never forget
memories of our parents.

*Omokage wo
utsushi todomuru
waza mo naki
yo ni usetarishi
oya wo koso omoe*

(See pp. *40-41*)

折にふれて

もろこしのはたの高粱ふく風に霜ちる夜はのさむさをぞおもふ

◇明治三十七年（1904年）

＊中国の東北部などで多く栽培されているモロコシの一種。当時満洲が日露戦争の戦場となっていた。

222

On Occasion

How cold it must be
the night when, across the fields
of tall sorghum corn,*
the frost, driven by the wind,
is being blown all away.

*Morokoshi no
hata no takakibi
fuku kaze ni
shimo chiru yowa no
samusa wo zo omou*

*Sorghum is a corn growing in Manchuria where the Imperial troops were fighting during the Russo-Japanese War.

夜聞水声

かきねゆくながれあるらし夜にいりて着きたるやどに水のおとする

◇明治三十七年（1904年）

Listening to the Sound of Water at Night

It seems a small stream
is running alongside
the fence of hedges;
arriving at our lodge at night
we hear the sound of water.

Kakine yuku
nagare arurashi
yo ni irite
tsukitaru yado ni
mizu no oto suru

思故郷

宮のうちにまねる世しらでふるさとの家にありつる昔こひしも

◇明治三十七年（1904年）

Thinking of Our Home

Without knowing
we would someday ascend
to dwell here at Court,
those past days we lived at home
are still so very cherished.

Miya-no-uchi ni
mairu yo shirade
furusato no
ie ni aritsuru
mukashi koishi mo

董

里の子がつみしすみれのひとつかねみしらぬわれにおくるうれしさ

◇明治三十九年（1906年）

（十八頁参照）

Violet

A village child,
without knowing us at all,
granted us a gift
of a bouquet of violets,
bringing us much joy.

*Sato no ko ga
tsumishi sumire no
hito tsukane
mishiranu ware ni
okuru ureshisa*

(See p. *17*)

夜神楽

まもらししいくさの勝にみこころもすみまさるらし月の夜かぐら

◇明治三十九年（1906年）

*Night Kagura**

Upon the victory
protected by our deities,
His Majesty's heart
seems serene under the moon
at an evening of *Kagura*.

*Mamorashishi
ikusa no kachi ni
mi-kokoro mo
sumi masarurashi
tsuki no yo-kagura*

Kagura: Sacred Shinto Music

深夜夢

＊
ぬばたまの夜ぶかきゆめにみえにけり樺太島はかかるところか

からふとじま

＊
夜にかかる枕詞

◇明治三十九年（１９０６年）

232

Late Night Dream

In the darkness
of the middle of the night
we saw in a dream;
the Karafuto Island,*
might it be such a place?

Nubatama no
yo-bukaki yume ni
mienikeri
Karafuto-jima wa
kakaru tokoro ka

∗Karafuto: It is now called Sakhalin and is considered to be in Russian territory.

靖国神社にまうでて

神がきに涙たむけてをがむらしかへるをまちし親も妻子_{つまこ}も

◇明治三十九年（1906年）

Praying at the Yasukuni Shrine*

In front of the shrine
they seem to offer up their tears
as prayer of sadness;
how they longed for homecomings
these parents, wives and children.

*Kami-gaki ni
namida tamukete
ogamurashi
kaeru wo machishi
oya mo tsuma-ko mo*

*A shrine established by Emperor Meiji in 1869 to commemorate and to show appreciation and respect to those who dedicated their lives to their mother country.

おぼしめすことおほからむ大御代のみまつりごとのしげくなるにも

◇明治四十年（1907）

Recollections

His Majesty's concerns
over the Affairs of State
must be numerous;
there is so much now to govern
in His Glorious Reign.

Oboshimesu
koto ōkaran
ō-mi-yo no
mimatsuri-goto no
shigeku naru nimo

述懐

さまざまのものおもひせしのちにこそうれしきこともある世なりけれ

◇明治四十一年（1908年）

Recollections

Many many things
cause us to be troubled,
yet because of this
other things bring us real joy;
such is this world of ours.

Sama-zama no
mono omoiseshi
nochi ni koso
ureshiki koto mo
aru yo narikere

菊

あれましし日にささげむとおもふかなうゑし垣根の菊のはつ花

◇明治四十三年（1910年）

＊お誕生日

（二十三頁参照）

◇1910 (Meiji43)

Chrysanthemum

We wish to offer
as a Royal birthday gift
the very first bloom
of the hedgerow chrysanthemum
we ourself had planted.

Aremashishi
hi ni sasagen to
omou kana
ueshi kakine no
kiku no hatsu-hana

(See p. *21*)

冬更衣

風寒みけふぬぎかへし冬ごろもたちゐもおもしおいにける身は

◇明治四十三年（1910年）

Changing into Winter Clothes

With the chilly wind
we changed our wardrobe today
into winter gowns;
it feels so heavy just to move
at the old age we've become.

Kaze samumi
kyō nugi-kaeshi
fuyu-goromo
tachii mo omoshi
oinikeru mi wa

往事如夢

こしかたはみな夢なれど君がためうれしかりつることはわすれず

◇明治四十三年（1910年）

244

The Past

Even though the past
is nothing more than a dream,
yet all those things
that brought His Majesty joy
shall never be forgotten.

Koshi kata wa
mina yume naredo
kimi ga tame
ureshikaritsuru
koto wa wasurezu

櫛

櫛のはにあまりし昔おもふかなすくなくなれる髪をときつつ

◇明治四十四年（1911年）

（四十七頁参照）

Comb

Teeth of our comb
bring memories of profusion
of the olden days
but now just a combing
shows how thin our hairs became.

> *Kushi no ha ni*
> *amarishi mukashi*
> *omou kana*
> *sukunaku nareru*
> *kami wo toki tsu-tsu*

(See pp. *50-51*)

惜落花

みいとまのあらむ日またで桜ばなをしくも風にちりみだれつつ*

◇明治四十五年（1912年）

*御用のないお時間

248

Regretting the Falling Flowers

Not waiting at all
for a day His Majesty
could view cherry blossoms,
we* so much regret a breeze
came blowing them all away.

Mi-itoma no
aran hi matade
sakura-bana
oshiku mo kaze ni
chiri-midare tsu-tsu

*Although the Empress often uses no pronoun at all in most of
these poems, since the subject is understood, it seems appropriate to
use the "royal we" or "majestic plural" ("we" instead of "I") when
needed, in these translations.

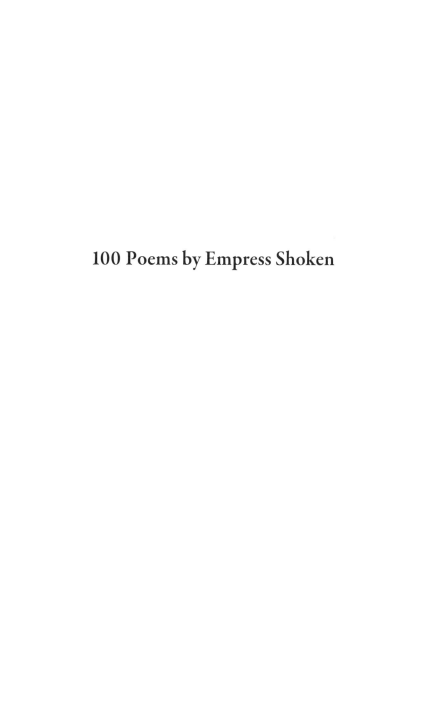

100 Poems by Empress Shoken

ハロルド・ライト

1931年アメリカ、オハイオ州生まれ。高校卒業後、海軍に入隊し、1952年に日本に派遣され、『万葉集』に出会う。除隊後、ハワイ大学へ進学し、日本文学（和歌）を専攻、さらに60年にコロンビア大学大学院に進んで、ドナルド・キーンに師事する。62年にはフルブライト奨学生に選ばれ、慶應義塾大学文学部に学ぶ。1964年、明治神宮が東京オリンピックに際して明治天皇と昭憲皇太后の和歌数種の英訳を企画し、ドナルド・キーンが翻訳者として著者を推薦した。1965年よりオハイオ州立大学やアンティオーク大学で教授を務める。アンティオーク大学名誉教授。2022年、『敷島の道に架ける橋——英語で伝えたい明治天皇百首』を刊行。

明治を綴る麗しの歌
——英語で伝えたい昭憲皇太后百首

2024年3月25日　初版発行

編　訳　　ハロルド・ライト
監　修　　明治神宮
発行者　　安部順一
発行所　　中央公論新社
　　　　　〒100-8152　東京都千代田区大手町1-7-1
　　　　　電話　販売 03-5299-1730　編集 03-5299-1740
　　　　　URL https://www.chuko.co.jp/

DTP　　　ハンズ・ミケ
印　刷　　図書印刷
製　本　　大口製本印刷

Harold Wright

Editorial oversight   Meiji Jingu Shrine

Meiji as Composed in Elegant Verse

100 Poems by Empress Shoken

Chuokoron-Shinsha

contents

Greetings from Meiji Jingu Shrine
Kujo Michinari   Chief Priest   5

Poetry of the Heart:
Waka Poetry of Empress Shoken
Harold Wright   Poetry-translator   9

commentary
30,000 Poems Reflecting The Heart
and Mind of the Empress   27
Nagata Koh   *Waka* poet, Cell biologist

100 Poems by Empress Shoken   53
—Japanese/English bilingual—

Photograph of Empress Shoken
Kuichi Uchida 1872

昭憲皇太后御写真
内田九一撮影（明治5年）

Greetings from Meiji Jingu Shrine

Kujo Michinari, Chief Priest

Bridge on the Shikishima Way —*100 Poems by Emperor Meiji* was published in the summer of 2022, the 110th anniversary year of the demise of Emperor Meiji. This year, April 2024, marks the 110th anniversary year of the demise of Empress Shoken, it has therefore been decided to release *Meiji as Composed in Elegant Verse* —*100 Poems by Empress Shoken,* at this time.

This publication is a source of great joy for Meiji Jingu, the place where the souls of Emperor Meiji and his consort Empress Shoken are enshrined. This new publication contains 100 poems selected from the approximately 30,000 poems written by Empress Shoken during her lifetime. It is my dearest hope that people who understand Japanese will be able to compare the elegant Japanese originals with their English translations, and that readers from an English-speaking background will be able to peruse the English translations, composed faithfully in the 5-7-5-7-7 meter of traditional Japanese poetry, and in

so doing experience something of the spirit of the poems and an appreciation of the essence of Japanese culture.

The story of how Prof. Harold Wright of the United States came to translate the poems of Emperor Meiji and Empress Shoken was touched upon at the time of the publication of 100 Poems by Emperor Meiji. After being approached by the Chief Priest of Meiji Jingu back in 1982, which was the year marking the 70th anniversary of the demise of Emperor Meiji, Prof. Wright spent great time and effort over the translation of the poems over the course of more than 30 years. I understand that translating into English *waka* poems, each of which expresses a uniquely Japanese sensibility within the confines of just 31 syllables, presents unimaginable difficulties to the translator. In publishing this new volume, Mr. Sato Masahiro, director of Meiji Intercultural Research Institute, as he did with the Emperor's book in 2022, took the lead in reviewing the poems, sharing the Empress' spirit that can be appreciated in each of them; then Prof. Wright, together with his wife Jonatha, recomposed the poems with English words and phrases that would most appropriately express the spirit. I hereby express my greatest esteem for Prof. Wright's insatiable inquisitiveness and passion for Japanese culture, which remains strong, even at the age of ninety-two.

Emperor Meiji and the Meiji Era that was named after him is remembered by many people for the brilliance of the

modernization that was achieved in such a short period of time, following the end of the Edo Shogunate. At the same time however, there are perhaps relatively few opportunities to reflect on the achievements of Empress Shoken during this momentous period of nation building. While respecting the traditions of the Imperial Family that had been protected and nurtured in the ancient capital of Kyoto for more than 1,000 years, the Empress was also a major proponent of change, and a source of warm encouragement and spiritual support for Emperor Meiji. For example, one cannot help but think that even the adoption of Western-style court dress at the Imperial Palace must have been achieved only with a great sense of determination. Empress Shoken's unique female perspective on Western culture and practices brought about by the opening of Japan is expressed in a number of her poems. Even now, it seems as if she is still gently speaking to us, sharing her thoughts on the promotion of domestic industry and girls' education, her desire to interact with people around the world and her peace-loving spirit.

What is still more moving are her poems filled with admiration and love for Emperor Meiji: her desire to cut flowers by hand and offer them to her husband, and her concern for the Emperor on his travels around the country. I truly hope that through this collection of poems, which were composed as if flowing from Empress Shoken's

innermost spirit as she accompanied Emperor Meiji through turbulent and fast-moving times, readers may be reminded of the compassion that exists in our own hearts, feel a sense of love and gratitude for nature, and also think of the *Yamato* spirit of Japan, which has been passed down through generations.

In closing I would like to reiterate my most heartfelt appreciation to Prof. Harold Wright for his long years of dedication to the English translation of the poems, and to his wife, Mrs. Jonatha Wright. I would also like to express my sincere gratitude to poetess Prof. Nagata Koh, for her contribution to the manuscript.

Poetry of the Heart
Waka Poetry of Empress Shoken

Harold Wright

Harold Wright

Harold Wright, born 1931 in the US city of Dayton, Ohio, eventually studied Japanese language and literature under Prof. Donald Keene at Columbia University. At the time of the 1964 Tokyo Olympics, he, as Fulbright Scholar of Japanese poetry at Keio University, was invited by Meiji Jingu to translate the first of many poems of Emperor Meiji and Empress Shoken. His other translations span from the ancient poetry of the Man'yoshu to the contemporary verse of Tanikawa Shuntaro. Presently, he is an Emeritus Professor of Japanese Language, Literature and Culture at Antioch College, Yellow Springs, Ohio, where he still resides with his wife Jonatha.

AS THE EMPRESS CONSORT OF MEIJI

Empress Shoken, Lady Masako Ichijo, was given the name Haruko (美子) upon her engagement to Emperor Meiji, in 1869. This name reflected her serene beauty and diminutive size. By the time of their Imperial wedding in 1869, delayed due to the political turmoil of the time, both Emperor Meiji and Empress Shoken had been writing *waka* poetry for years. *Waka*, also known as *tanka*, is the 31 syllable poetry form favored by Japanese poets since ancient times. Both the Emperor and the Empress began composing poetry at the age of five. During his lifetime the Emperor was said to have written close to one hundred thousand and the Empress thirty thousand of the short poems. Over the years they shared their poems with each other as well as the world outside the palace. An early example of her poetry goes:

Migakazuba
tama mo kagami mo
nanika sen
manabi no michi mo

kaku koso arikere

If left unpolished
neither jewels nor mirrors
are worth anything;
this is also very true
of the path of learning.

To quote the renowned Japanese scholar, Donald Keene: "The union of Meiji and his bride would not, as it happened, be blessed with children, but Haruko would be a far more prominent public figure than any consort for many hundreds of years." (*Emperor of Japan: Meiji and His World 1852-1912, page 108.*) Meiji's children, including his son, Emperor Taisho, were born to other aristocratic women as was the custom of the court at that time. The Emperor Meiji and Empress Shoken maintained a close relationship through their formal court appearances as well as shared private times as some of their poems indicate.

Aki goto ni
tsuranaru hito no
kazu soite
utage nigiwau
kiku no hanazono

VIEWING CHRYSANTHEMUMS (1886)

Every autumn now,
our invited guests of state
have grown in number;
we have a bustling banquet
in the chrysanthemum garden.

They even had their playful and deeply personal moments that were often expressed in poetry. Once she wrote:

Kimi ga tame
oran to sureba
kuro-kami no
ue ni midarete
chiru sakura kana

CHERRY BLOSSOMS (1880)

Breaking off a branch
of the blooming cherry
for His Majesty,
petals of flowers are scattered
over our long black locks.

Like her husband, Empress Shoken's worldview was one of curiosity, open mindedness and international friendliness. She was an innovator in wearing Western clothes. "The New Year ceremonies at the beginning of 1887 followed tradition in all but one respect: the Empress wore a formal Western gown when accepting congratulations from members of the court, and this became her normal costume for such occasions."(*Keene, p. 411*).

She had first appeared in Western clothes in public when she attended the graduation ceremony at the Peeresses' School on July 30, 1886. Afterwards the Empress maintained that Western clothes were more suitable for meeting foreign dignitaries and guests than Japanese kimonos.

Also she was fascinated with Western products such as writing slates and the telegraph.

Kaku moji no
tsutanaki ato mo
todomaranu
ishi no fude koso
ureshikarikere

SLATE PENCILS (1892)

Even if we wrote
something in an unskilled hand
it could be erased;
oh, these "stone writing brushes"
bring us joy of easiness.

Agata-mori
osamuru michi mo
hito-suji ni
tsuge matsuru beki
ito-guchi ya kore

TELEGRAPH (before 1879)

How do heads of regions
now report to central office,
the ways they govern?
The clue is in just one thing:
a single thread of wire.

THREE TYPES OF POETRY SHARED BY THE EMPEROR AND EMPRESS

Empress Shoken, like the Emperor, wrote poetry in such categories as follows:

The first is what I call Imperial Poetry. It is written from the point of view of being a caring and nurturing member of the royal family to the people of Japan and her concern for the nation as a whole. Here are three examples:

Shiroshimesu
Ō-mi-kunuchi ni
koto nakute
kururu toshi koso
nodokekarikere

END OF THE YEAR (1884)
The whole country
under His Majesty's reign
has remained at peace;
and, indeed, the end of this year
is truly calm and tranquil.

Ikabakari
ureshikaruran
yurusarete
mi-kawa no mizu wo
oda ni hiku hi wa

WATER ON THE 22ND OF MAY (1897)

How happy they must be
the day when farmers are allowed
to draw in water
from the stream in the palace grounds
to flood their own fields of rice.

Sato no ko ga
tsumishi sumire no
hito tsukane
mishiranu ware ni
okuru ureshisa

VIOLET (1906)

A village child,
without knowing us at all,
granted us a gift
of a bouquet of violets,
bringing us much joy.

A second category she and the Emperor shared is
Shinto Poems. This poetry reflects the Empress' position
as the wife of the head of the Shinto religion and the belief
that his ancestors reach back to the Age of *Kami:*

*Kami-kaze no
Ise no uchito no
miya-bashira
yuruginaki yo wo
nao inoru kana*

PRAYERS AT THE ISE SHRINE FOR THE REIGN (1891)

At Sacred Ise
we pray at both the Inner
and the Outer Shrines
that, like their pillars,
our reign shall never waver.

A third category they shared, I believe, might be called Personal Poems, or the poems that simply spring from their emotions deep within their hearts as poets. Personal poems the Empress wrote often speak of her pleasant memories of and joy in remembering her and the Emperor's childhood home, in Kyoto, the old capital; her love of nature, especially plants, flowers, birds and water; her thirst for knowledge and especially her deep satisfaction with and love of writing.

Kaze wo itami

kamo wa tachinishi
misabie ni
uwage bakari zo
chiriukabitaru

   WINTER BAY (1890)

As strong winds blew
all the ducks just flew away
from murky waters,
leaving nothing there at all
but scattered floating feathers.

Their desire for world peace and international understanding is a theme of poetry shared by the Emperor and the Empress as well. This is one of Empress Shoken's examples:

Moto wa mina
onaji nezashi no
hitogusa mo
kotoba no hana ya
chiji ni sakuran

   UNIVERSAL BROTHERHOOD (1882)

In the beginning

people, like all of our plants,
sprang from one root,
followed by flowers of language
blooming forth by the thousands.

TWO TYPES PARTICULAR TO THE EMPRESS' POEMS

In addition to these categories that she and the
Emperor shared, I believe that Empress Shoken wrote in
two additional themes or categories. One is a large group
of personal poems about her husband, Emperor Meiji. She
expresses her admiration for him, and was proud of his
numerous accomplishments. Many of these poems were
written out of her deep concern for his welfare, especially
during his many official travels around Japan for important
meetings, various official ceremonies and when he was
observing the well-being of his subjects. They could not
communicate quickly, with the exceptions of the telegraph,
and messages delivered by train. She was often very anxious
about treacherous roads he traveled, extreme weather
conditions and his general comfort.

Mi-kuruma wo
matsu ma hisashiki
yūyami ni
mune todorokasu

ame no oto kana

HIS MAJESTY'S TRAVEL IN THE RAIN (1883)
Waiting so long
for His Majesty's carriage
here at nightfall,
this heart of ours is throbbing
to the sounds of the rain.

Aremashishi
hi ni sasagen to
omou kana
ueshi kakine no
kiku no hatsu-hana

CHRYSANTHEMUM (1910)
We wish to offer
as a Royal birthday gift
the very first bloom
of the hedgerow chrysanthemum
we ourself had planted.

The Empress also wrote a series of poems inspired by America's Benjamin Franklin's "The Book of Virtues."

It is an accepted story that the Empress Shoken had learned from her tutor Motoda Nagazane, that Benjamin Franklin of the United States, highly valued the following virtues:

Temperance, cleanliness, industry, silence, resolution, sincerity, moderation, humility, order, frugality, tranquility and justice

In 1994, Emperor Akihito made an official visit to the United States. Bill Clinton was president. When speaking at the White House, Emperor Akihito repeated this story about Empress Shoken's tutor having introduced her to Franklin's "Virtues."

Here is her poem on the virtue, Humility:

Taka-yama no
kage wo utsushite
yuku mizu no
hikiki ni tsuku wo
kokoro to mogana

HUMILITY *(before 1879)*
The lofty mountains
are carried in reflection
by flowing waters;
this seeking of humble levels

should be the aim of human hearts.

There is a physical description of her appearance from an American teacher of English at the Peeresses' School for Japanese girls, Alice Mabel Bacon, whose classroom the Empress visited.

> "I had caught several good glimpses of her... These glimpses revealed a small, slender woman...rather loaded down by her heavy dove-colored silk dress and dove-colored Paris bonnet with a white plume. Her face seemed to me a sad one, with a patient look about it.... They say that she is a very intellectual woman, and one of great strength and beauty of character."
>
> (*"A Japanese Interior," Bacon, Alice Mabel, British Historical Print Editions, British Library, 1893*)

The Empress met many Western leaders and their wives over the years. In 1881 she met the Hawaiian King Kalakaua. Also that year she met the sons of future British King Edward VII. She hosted the wife of former President Grant, Julia Dent Grant, during the Grants' visit to Japan at the end of their world tour, after his presidency, in1879. Mrs. Grant in her autobiography, "The Personal Memoirs

of Julia Dent Grant" wrote:

> "Their Majesties were standing. The Emperor was dressed in uniform, the Empress in a court robe of ruby velvet over a white silk skirt. Her hair was dressed in beautiful, wide plaits arranged in a large jeweled coronet or, rather, an aigrette, resembling the end of a peacock feather. The Empress was young and fair and delicate-looking. She said a few words of welcome to me through an interpreter, to which I made a suitable reply."

At another meeting the Empress was speaking with Mrs. Grant and expressing concern about the Grants' exhausting journey in very hot weather. To this Mrs. Grant replied: "...by declaring that in none of the many countries she and her husband had visited were they treated with such great kindness as in Japan." *(Keene, p. 313.)*

IN CONCLUSION

All in all, it has been a wonderful and humbling opportunity to be involved in this attempt to translate the rich poetry of the Empress Shoken, beginning with the request I received from Chief Priest Takasawa of Meiji Jingu, at the time of the 1964 Olympics.

Over the years, I have become more and more grateful to many people for their insight into not only the meaning of these beautiful poems, but also the many ways of expressing such poetic sentiments in English.

For my previous published book of Imperial poetry translations, *"Bridge on the Shikishima Way —100 Poems by Emperor Meiji, (Chuokoron-Shinsha, August 2022)*, I was asked to write of my own history of involvement with the translation process into English of the Imperial poetry. Please refer to my earlier book, where I explain my translation process in detail. I see no need to repeat myself here.

Foremost I wish to thank Mr. Masahiro Sato, Director of the Intercultural Research Institute at Meiji Jingu and his untiring staff, at the end of our e-mail link in Tokyo. And here in Ohio my gratitude goes out to my poet wife, Jonatha Hammer Wright, who patiently discussed with me every word and idea in this book. At my own age of 92, I find her still youthful vigor and feminine insights an indispensable aid in the fulfillment of this cross-cultural task.

I would also like to thank everyone everywhere who joined me in an enthusiastic conversation about Japan and

its rich culture of poetry. There are many, among them: teachers, students, people I love, writers of books, even strangers on mountain trails and fellow passengers on long train rides. All of you have participated in aiding me in appreciating everything that has gone in the making of this book. You have all helped me to live a wonderful life of trying to translate Japanese Poetry into this puzzling language we call English.

Doumo arigatou gozaimasu

Harold Wright

Migakazuba, a Poem Composed and Handwritten by Empress Shoken
（English translation, p.57）［Ochanomizu University］

御歌御色紙 ［お茶の水女子大学所蔵］
昭憲皇太后が「みがかずば」という御題で詠まれた御歌（56頁参照）

Court Dress worn
by Empress Shoken
[©Daishoji, Photo by Morio Kanai]

昭憲皇太后大礼服
[大聖寺蔵　金井杜道撮影]

Multitiered Writing Box in Mulberry Wood with Maki-e Lacquerwork
[Meiji Jingu Museum]

桑木地蒔絵　御重硯 [明治神宮ミュージアム所蔵]
昭憲皇太后が御歌会の節にご使用になった六段重ねの硯箱

Commentary
30,000 Poems Reflecting the Heart and Mind of the Empress
Nagata Koh, *Waka* poet/Cell biologist

Upon hearing the name of Empress Shoken, perhaps the first thing that comes to mind is a portrait of a woman in ceremonial court dress, resplendent in a tiara fringed with star-shaped diamonds. As can be seen in the photograph that was taken in June 1889, Empress Shoken was the first Empress of Japan to wear Western dress. In an era of rapid Westernization and advancing modernization, Empress Shoken is known for her great achievements in women's education and social welfare, while concurrently responding to the dramatic changes in society as the consort of Emperor Meiji. Throughout the course of her eventful life, Empress Shoken composed some 30,000 *waka* poems.

Empress Shoken was born into the Ichijo family, one of the distinguished Five Regent Houses, and her childhood home was located just one street away from Kyoto Imperial Palace. Living in central Kyoto myself, the Kyoto Gyoen National Garden, where the Imperial Palace is located, was a familiar place to me in my childhood, and somewhere I always feel at ease whenever I visit, in all seasons of the year.

Looking around the world it always seems that the cities that are the most comfortable places to live are always those that have a river and nice parks, and I always feel happy that Kyoto is similarly blessed with the Kamogawa River and Kyoto Gyoen National Garden.

In the northwest corner of the garden is a children's park built on the site of the former Konoe family residence, where my elementary school-age daughter goes to play. Just to the southwest of that park is the site of the old Ichijo family residence. While watching my daughter play on the swings with their acorn and owl motifs, I am reminded once again that this is where Empress Shoken spent her early years, before entering the Imperial Family. The Nakayama Residence, where Emperor Meiji spent his childhood, is located on the east side of the Konoe Residence, and it never ceases to astonish me how close to each other the Emperor and Empress lived during their formative years.

Walking along the gravel path of the garden, a large and beautiful gingko tree at the site of the Ichijo residence catches the eye. It is unclear how old this tree is, but I sometimes like to imagine that Empress Shoken perhaps also looked at this tree as she grew up in her family home. This volume includes a poem that reads as follows.

Mukashi waga
mi wo hiroinishi

furusato no
kashi no ōki wa
ima mo nokoreri
(1902)

Long, long ago
we would gather acorns
in the old hometown;
even today it still stands
the gigantic oak tree.

It would appear that Empress Shoken enjoyed collecting acorns from an oak tree, but I wonder whether the gingko tree was already growing there at that time. It is a place that I have often walked past without thinking until now, but after reading Empress Shoken's poem carefully, it gives me pause and I now stop to gaze.

A woman born in this place more than 170 years ago; there is no doubt that the days Empress Shoken spent in Kyoto nurtured her character and sensitiveness. Even after leaving Kyoto for Tokyo, one cannot help but imagine how she must have longed for this place, thinking of the mountains she could see from her family home. On the site of where the residence garden once stood there is still a well, known as *Agatai*, from which it is said water was drawn for

Empress Shoken's first bath as a newborn baby. Next to the well were the scattered white petals of a *camellia*.

At birth Empress Shoken was given the name Masako, and during her childhood she was known as Fuki-gimi, which was later changed to Sue-gimi. Her mother passed away when she was nine, and her father succumbed to illness when she was 14. She was selected to become Emperor Meiji's bride and just before entering the Imperial Family was bestowed the name Haruko. She entered the Imperial Family on February 9, 1869, when Emperor Meiji was 16 years old and she was herself 18 years old. Following her demise in 1914 she was given the posthumous name of Empress Shoken. She had no children with Emperor Meiji.

Empress Shoken's father, Ichijo Tadaka, was passionate about children's education. It is said that from an early age the Empress was made to read the Four Books and Five Classics, as well as Japanese and Chinese literature, in addition to which her father constructed a watch tower, from which his children might observe the lives of ordinary citizens. Her poetry teacher was Konoe Tadahiro.

Although not included in this collection, Empress Shoken composed the following poem.

Neko no ko wo
hiza ni oki tsu-tsu
fumi yomishi

osana-gokoro mo
yume to nariniki
(1901)

Cuddling a kitten
close to us on our lap
while we read a book…
Even the heart of childhood
has gone the way of dreams.

It describes an idyllic scene, where as a young girl
she would sit reading with a kitten curled up on her lap.
While sensing the soft fur and body warmth of the kitten,
she enters the world of books and yearns for a world she has
yet to see, a young girl immersed in reading her books with
a heart filled with excitement for the future that is about to
unfold. She was a great reader and studious, and is said to
have remarked in later years, "There is no greater pleasure
than the pleasure to be had from reading books." The poem
above was composed after Empress Shoken turned 50
years old, and expresses her feeling that the halcyon days of
childhood are now so far away as if to be a dream. Reading
her warm and tactile memories of her childhood days, I am
reminded of a gentleness that lights up her life.

Yoru hikaru
tama mo nanisen
mi wo terasu
fumi koso hito no
takara narikere

Those precious jewels
even ones that glow at night
are not worth anything.
That which brightens up our lives
are the treasures of reading.

    This poem speaks about how books are a shining treasure that light up a person more than any glittering jewels ever could. You really get a sense of Empress Shoken's deep trust in books and learning. After becoming Empress she was also a keen advocate of education for girls, most likely because she had experienced for herself just how greatly learning can expand a person's world.

    She was a supporter of and frequent visitor to Tokyo Women's Normal School (present-day Ochanomizu University) and the Peeresses' School (present-day Gakushuin Girls' Junior & Senior High School) and gifted poems to both institutions. These poems would subsequently be put to music, and are still sung today as the

schools' songs.

The poem that she gifted to Tokyo Women's Normal School in February 1876 was *Migakazuba* (*"If Left Unpolished"*).

> *Migakazuba*
> *tama mo kagami mo*
> *nanika sen*
> *manabi no michi mo*
> *kaku koso arikere*

> If left unpolished
> neither jewels nor mirrors
> are worth anything;
> this is also very true
> of the path of learning.

Jewels and mirrors are nothing unless polished. The path of learning is just the same. In order to be able to shine, one must continue to apply oneself to study and self-improvement.

In March 1887, Empress Shoken gifted two poems to the Peeresses' School, *Kongōseki* (*Diamond*), and *Mizu wa Utsuwa* (*As Water Requires a Container*). It is said that when these poems were read out for the first time, it was

Empress Shoken herself who read them from the podium in a high voice that seemed to echo throughout the room.

Kongōseki
Even a diamond when not polished,
Beautiful light will not be refracted
People, as well, only after learning,
Gain true virtue
The hands on a timepiece rotate without pause,
As periods of time roll by
Working hard without wasting daylight,
Leads to a splendid outcome

Mizu wa Utsuwa
As Water Requires a Container
Adapting to containers,
Water becomes variously shaped
According to the friends one has,
One appears better or worse
Good friends who surpass me,
For those I seek to select
I will whip my mind as if it were a horse,
As I proceed along the path of learning
[translation reference : *"Taisetsuna Koto"* (Meiji Jingu)]

The meaning of these poems is plain to see. Similarly to *If Left Unpolished*, *Diamond* teaches the need to strive for constant self-improvement. *As Water Requires a Container* reminds us that just as water changes its shape depending on the vessel it is in, people can also change for better or worse depending on the friends they have, so it is a source of warm encouragement to have a better person than yourself as a friend, and to be strict with yourself on the path of learning.

Each of these works symbolically expresses the essential nature of things and are persuasive in their composition. The Empress must have given careful thought to how the metaphor would resonate with young female students. They are also words of self-discipline, derived from quiet introspection into her own heart and mind.

In actual fact, from among the 12 poems that Empress Shoken composed that are known to be based on the *Twelve Virtues of Benjamin Franklin*, there is this one, titled *Industry*.

Migakazuba
tama no hikari wa
idezaran
hito no kokoro mo
kaku koso arurashi
(Before 1879)

If left unpolished
the glow of precious stones
will not luster forth;
it must also be quite true
of these human hearts of ours.

If we compare this poem with *If Left Unpolished* described above, although "jewels and mirrors" have been replaced by the "glow of precious stones," and the "path of learning" by "these human hearts of ours," the exhortation remains the same, namely the will to apply oneself diligently to study and strive for self-improvement. Empress Shoken entered the Imperial Family as the bride of Emperor Meiji, who had acceded to the throne at a young age, and in so doing she became Empress consort without ever having been Crown Princess. Accordingly, she had no time to prepare, nor did she benefit from a period during which she could observe and learn from the works of the previous Empress. It is hard to imagine how heavy a responsibility and lonely it must have been to suddenly find oneself elevated to the position of Empress. Without any role model, she had to create by her own hand an image of an Empress befitting the new era.

In 1876 Motoda Nagazane, an Imperial tutor, had offered a lecture to Empress Shoken about the twelve virtues

enumerated by Benjamin Franklin, one of the authors of the American Declaration of Independence. In other words, Motoda introduced the twelve virtues that Franklin had specifically listed as necessary for cultivating his own character, including, "temperance," "cleanliness," "industry," "justice," and so on. The Empress must have been under immense and constant pressure to elucidate the right role for an Empress in what were fast-changing and tumultuous times. It was just at this time that she encountered Franklin's twelve virtues, and translated them into *waka* poetry form. I believe that the process of translating the text into the Japanese language helped the Empress to internalize the essence of these virtues, make sense of them and become convinced of their truth.

These poems were subsequently printed in national school textbooks and became widely known by the public. All twelve are included in this collection.

In those days, *waka* poetry of the Imperial court was subject to the strictly observed rule that only words that appeared in the *Kokin Wakashū* (*Collection of Japanese Poems of Ancient and Modern Times* compiled in the 10th century) were permissible for use in poems. It must have been immensely challenging to compose poems while living in the Meiji era, a time when new culture and cultural goods and items were appearing in a seemingly never-ending flow.

This volume includes some of the Empress' poems that were based on the new cultural items that were being brought into Japan from the West.

Agata-mori
osamuru michi mo
hito-suji ni
tsuge matsuru beki
ito-guchi ya kore
(Before 1879)

How do heads of regions
now report to the central office,
the ways they govern?
The clue is in just one thing:
a single thread of wire.

Chiru nami no
iro no mizu nite
hana-moji mo
kaki-nagasu yo to
narinikeru kana
(1886)

Using water

in colors of splashing waves
we write fluidly
in florid calligraphy;
such is our world today.

Tomoshibi no
hikari wo karite
totsu-kuni no
shiranu no-yama mo
miru yo narikeri
(1899)

By using the light
of just the flame of a lamp
we view fields and mountains
of lands never seen before.
This is our world of today.

Each of these poems had a title, but I wonder if you can imagine to what it is each one refers? The first one is about the "telegraph" one of the advanced technologies of the time, including telegrams, telegraph wires, and telegraph machines. In actual fact it was Commodore Perry, who had brought the telegraph machine and telegraph wires to

Japan, when he appeared in his "black ships" seeking the opening of Japan. The first telegraph wire in Japan was installed in 1869. In the poem the Empress was unable to use the proscribed characters for telegraph wire, and it is extremely interesting that she chose instead to refer to it as a "single *thread* of wire." The second poem is about "ink," which is referred to as "water in colors." The third poem is about a "magic lantern," an early image projector. It must have been deeply moving to realize that technology had progressed to a point where it was possible to see the wilds and mountains of never-before-seen foreign countries using this magic lantern machine. As seen in both the second and third poems, where the Empress writes "such/this is our world of today," it is vividly clear that she is writing about the changing times inspired by a variety of different feelings.

> *Omokage wo*
> *utsushi todomuru*
> *waza mo naki*
> *yo ni usetarishi*
> *oya wo koso omoe*
> *(1903)*

> They lived in an age
> when we could not keep
> images of them;

so we should never forget
memories of our parents.

The "keeping images" in this poem refers to "photographs." It tells us that the Empress is thinking of her parents who passed away at a time when there was no photographic technology capable of capturing and saving their images.

Although not included in this volume, there are other poems by the Empress about photographs, which also make a deep impression.

Tarachine no
oya no mikage mo
nokoramashi
kono utsushi-e no
aru yo nariseba
(1888)

Images of parents
could have been kept for us
if they had just lived
in this world of ours today
with taking of pictures.

Nii-goromo
imada kinarenu
waga sugata
utsuhi todomuru
kage zo yasashiki
(1889)

We feel timid
when viewing the photograph
of our wearing
a new style Western gown
to which we're not accustomed.

"Utsushi-e" or "realistic picture" was originally a poetic word used to convey a sense of "a picture that resembles reality," or "a realistic picture," but by the Meiji era its meaning as "photograph" had become established. In this poem Empress Shoken laments the fact that she has no photographs of her parents, writing that if only it had been a time when photograph existed, she would have had some means of preserving her parents' images. She also conveys a sense of regret at having lost her parents at a young age. The second poem is from the time the Empress was photographed in an official portrait, wearing ceremonial

court dress and the tiara referred to above. The "new clothes" refer to Western dress, and the Empress records her "timidity," conveying to the reader her perplexity at the sight of her own dress, which she was neither yet accustomed to wearing nor to seeing.

Empress Shoken was not afraid to use the new cultural items and innovations as the subjects of her poems, including everything from trains, to telephones, airplanes, newspapers, perfume, western studies, telescopes, shoes, overseas travel, kindergartens, and equal rights for men and women. These words are not directly included in the *waka* poems, but are rather positioned as a title. I would surmise that perhaps Empress Shoken found some degree of amusement in the process of devising ways to express these new things in the Japanese language.

During his lifetime Emperor Meiji composed approximately 100,000 poems, and Empress Shoken is believed to have penned approximately 30,000, making them both astonishingly prolific poets. Although a simple calculation may provide us with an estimate of how many poems were composed during a single day on average, the power of such numbers is a perhaps surprisingly important element when it comes to writing poetry.

As a poetess myself, I feel that the more poems I compose, the easier it becomes to unleash my creativity. In

the process of composing many, many poems, it becomes easier to express a sense of one's own "reality" in the poems. At the same time, a part of oneself that one has not yet been made aware of may make itself apparent in the verse. The fact that both of these seemingly contradictory things occur constitutes one of the mysteries and also the allure of the creative process.

Of her sixty-five year life, Empress Shoken spent forty-five of those years by Emperor Meiji's side. It would not be wrong to speculate that it was precisely because the Imperial couple composed poems together that a synergistic effect was generated that inspired the creation of so many poems. *Waka* poetry does possess an aspect of calling out to one another, and whether we realize it or not, we respond in some way to the person close to us who is composing the poem. Feelings one has for the other person therefore naturally find expression in the form of a poem.

> *Ōmiya no*
> *uchi ni arite mo*
> *atsuki hi wo*
> *ikanaru yama ka*
> *kimi wa koyuran*
> (Before 1879)

On such a hot day

even inside the palace;
we are most concerned
over those mountains that
His Majesty is crossing.

Ōmiya no
tobari mo shimeru
asa-giri ni
kimi ga koyuran
yama-ji wo zo omou
(1880)

With morning fog
leaving even curtains damp
here in the palace,
we think of His Majesty
journeying on those mountain roads!

The first of these poems describes the Empress'
thoughts for the Emperor who was on a journey to Koshiji.
On such a hot day even in the palace, the Empress' thoughts
stray to the Emperor, as she wonders what mountain he
may be traversing. Although the Japanese original does
not explicitly refer to any words about "care," "concern,"

or "worry," the English version very precisely inserts "we are most concerned." It is eye-opening indeed to see the thoughts of the Empress that are imbued in the Japanese word *"ikanaru"* ("whatever" or "whichever") expressed in English in this way. The second poem also conveys the Empress' thoughts about a journey of the Emperor, but in this one *"omou"* in the Japanese is translated faithfully as "think," but given an extra emotional touch with the addition of an exclamation mark at the end of the sentence. In both of these poems we can sense the compassion of the Empress as she waits "inside the palace" or "here in the palace." While there is a sense of longing in those phrases, by composing a poem in this way she is able to bring the presence of the Emperor a little closer.

It is truly daunting to think of the difficulties that must be experienced when translating a *waka* poem written in Japanese into English. Poetry is a form that not only consists of the meaning of the words on the page, but also comprises a complex interplay of phrasing, rhyme, word order, and rhythm, among other factors. Moreover, it is sometimes important to have the courage to imbue words that are not intended to have meaning with some kind of poetic sentiment. Prof. Harold Wright, who translated 100 of Emperor Meiji's poems, has written in detail about the difficulties of translating *waka* poems and the translation process in "A Tale of a Translator" in his previous

publication *Bridge on the Shikishima Way* —*100 Poems by Emperor Meiji* (Chuokoron-Shinsha). There he notes that he worked for more than one year on a certain poem by Emperor Meiji.

Among translators there are those who set aside all poetic sentiment and translate only the meaning into monotonous sentences, and there are also those who, in contrast, are overly concerned with rhyme. Positioned between those two extremes, Prof. Wright notes that, "Translation of poetry is a tightrope circus act; it is easy to fall off one side or the other." I am sure that he set about the translation of these poems with just such a sense of tense awareness.

Let us also take a glance at some poems the Empress composed about Emperor Meiji himself.

Kimi ga tame
oran to sureba
kuro-kami no
ue ni midarete
chiru sakura kana
(1880)

Breaking off a branch
of the blooming cherry
for His Majesty,

petals of flowers are scattered
over our long black locks.

Kimi ga tame
erabite orishi
hito-eda ni
omoishi yori wa
hana no sukunaki
(1892)

Selecting a small branch
to present to His Majesty,
and breaking it off,
we could see, then, the blooms
were fewer than we believed.

The first one relates how the Empress reaches out to break off a high branch of a cherry tree. Just shaking the branch only slightly results in the flower petals fluttering down. The Empress' feelings for the Emperor are thus likened to the aesthetic beauty of the cherry blossom petals scattered in the black locks of the Empress. The second poem implies a sense of regret that the branch the Empress broke off for the Emperor had fewer blossoms on it than

she expected. Nonetheless, this sparseness of blossoms has a certain charm of its own.

Among Empress Shoken's poems, those that have a moral or instructive theme have been most widely shared and are best known, including *If Left Unpolished*, *Diamond*, and *As Water Requires a Container*. These all describe formal situations or notions (*hare-no-uta*) and of course all of these have profound significance. On the other hand, Empress Shoken also composed many poems about the minutiae of ordinary life (*ke-no-uta*), which are deeply atmospheric. Those poems, which describe plants in careful detail leave a deep impression on the reader.

Oi-matsu no
utsuho to nareru
uchi ni sae
sumire hana saku
furusato no niwa
(1892)

Even hollow places
in trunks of ancient pine trees
are growing clumps
of violet in the gardens
of our home of long ago.

Here the Empress writes about the violets blooming in hollow trunks of trees in the gardens of her family home. It is these small details that evoke a sense of nostalgia and longing.

Sue-okishi
kagami wasurete
waga kage wo
tareka to omou
toki mo arikeri
(1888)

Having forgotten
our mirror had been placed there,
it happened that
we wondered who the person was
when viewing our own reflection.

Kushi no ha ni
amarishi mukashi
omou kana
sukunaku nareru
kami wo toki tsu-tsu

(1911)

Teeth of our comb
bring memories of profusion
of the olden days
but now just a combing
shows how thin our hair became.

In this first poem the Empress for an instant fails
to recognize her own reflection in a mirror. In the second
poem, while combing her thinning hair, the Empress recalls
the past, when her luxuriant locks would almost overwhelm
the teeth of the comb. Both of these poems describe
situations that many of us can relate to. It is surprising how
candidly and clearly she writes about her own advancing
years, but perhaps the medium of poetry brings with it a
certain sense of comfort and ease.

While one might tend to think of persons of exalted
rank as being unapproachable and distant, *waka* is a poetic
form capable of reaching out across all worldly concerns
and touching our hearts directly.

I am truly happy that the English translation of 100
of Empress Shoken's poems will be shared with the world
this spring, and it is my dearest wish that this collection
touches the hearts of many people.

.